C000143125

BLOOD GROUP O

Also by David Brierley

Big Bear, Little Bear

The Cody Series
Cold War
Blood Group O
Skorpion's Death
Snowline
Death & Co.

BLOOD GROUP O

DAVID BRIERLEY

BRASH
BOOKS

Copyright © 2023 by David Brierley

The characters and events portrayed in this book are fictitious. Any similarity to real persons, living or dead, is coincidental and not intended by the author. No part of this book may be reproduced, or stored in a retrieval system, or transmitted in any form or by any means, electronic, mechanical, photocopying, recording, or otherwise, without express written permission of the publisher.

ISBN: 978-1-954841-74-1

Published by
Brash Books
PO Box 8212
Calabasas, CA 91372
www.brash-books.com

Don't argue, destroy
Gudrun Ensslin

PROLOGUE: PALMA, MOGADISHU, STAMMHEIM

It was on Thursday 13 October 1977.

The two men wore lightweight slacks, open-necked shirts and leather boots, brown with Cuban heels. The two women wore casual jackets and slacks. They looked and behaved much the same as the other people in the departure lounge, standing in a little group, exchanging few words, waiting for Flight 181 to be announced. If they showed any tension, it passed unnoticed.

The Spanish authorities didn't take security at Palma airport seriously. There was no electronic detector equipment, no manual searches were made, no women police officers were even available to carry out body checks on women passengers.

Some time past midday the eighty-seven passengers filed out to the Boeing 737. It was hot from standing in the sun. Captain Jürgen Schumman received TO clearance from Palma Control Tower and at 12.55 local time the Lufthansa flight was airborne. Flying time to Frankfurt was estimated at two hours fifteen minutes. Lunch would be served on board.

As the aircraft overflew the island of Elba, the two men took pistols from their leather boots. The women produced grenades, removing the priming pins. The men broke through to the flight deck and took command of LH181. The time was logged: 13.33.

That was the beginning.

Most commercial aircraft, the Lufthansa jet included, carry a hijack alarm, a switch that automatically broadcasts a distress signal through the transponder to air traffic controllers. Switching this on can easily be covered in the dozens of operations necessary to flying the machine, but Captain Schumman made no use of it. He knew from the reading of past hijacks that the net result was that airports blocked their runways. Nobody wants a hijacked plane on their hands.

ATC Nice were the first to note something amiss when the Lufthansa jet changed course from its filed flight plan. It turned south, followed the Italian coastline, touching down at Rome on runway 3 at 16.10. It taxied to a position some way off from the passenger terminal buildings at Fiumicino airport and waited. Carabinieri and armoured vehicles surrounded the plane. The men and women now in charge on board changed into red T-shirts with Che Guevara's head stencilled in black across the front. The leader, identifying himself as Captain Mahmoud or sometimes as Martyr Mahmoud, made their demands: the release of eleven prisoners in Germany, of two Arabs imprisoned in Turkey and several million dollars' ransom. At 17.40 the plane took off again.

In succession it landed at Larnaca in Cyprus (where there was an abortive meeting with a Palestinian Liberation leader whom the hijackers considered a traitor), Bahrain (where it refuelled and took on food and water) and Dubai. At Dubai it spent over two days. The demands were repeated under threats of blowing up the plane. The monotony of waiting was broken when three women passengers were beaten up: they were Jews.

On Sunday the plane took off and headed for Aden where, with the runway blocked by fire tenders, it made a forced landing on a dirt strip. The plane refuelled and spent some ten hours there before leaving with the co-pilot Victor at the controls. Shortly after take-off the Lufthansa Captain Schumann was accused of helping the enemy, and after a revolutionary trial in front of the passengers he was ordered to kneel and was shot in the head by Mahmoud. The body was left lying in the aisle of the cabin.

In the early hours of Monday morning the plane landed at Mogadishu airport in the Horn of Africa and another day of negotiations began. The heat and humidity were intense and conditions on board by now disgusting. ("The toilet is overflowing." "Then shit in your seat." The hijackers spoke English to the passengers, Arabic among themselves.) The eighty-three passengers, four hijackers and remaining four crew waited. In the afternoon it appeared the end had been reached: the hijackers used the women's nylons to tie up the male passengers and soaked the carpet with duty-free liquor and kerosene.

"You know what happens to passengers when a plane is blown up," Mahmoud said. "You fry."

The younger of the two women hijackers was humming as she emptied bottles of perfume that would add to the conflagration. She agreed that, as a humanitarian gesture, a four-year-old boy should be shot rather than burned to death. Finally a message was relayed that the hijacker's demands were going to be met by the West German government and tension eased.

Still they waited.

Hours dragged while the German authorities completed negotiations with Somalia. Chancellor Schmidt spent over an hour in personal telephone conversation with President Barre. Eventually, permission for an operation at Mogadishu airport was given in return for the promise of increased German economic aid. Under cover of darkness, with landing lights doused and only a weak moon to see by, a German Boeing 707 carrying sixty members of Grenzschutzgruppe 9 landed.

Arrangements were finalized. It was to be an exclusively German operation with no Somali participation except in a background role. The Germans insisted on that: preparations for a similar operation at Dubai had broken down because of the blundering presence of local troops.

The codeword was "Otto".

GSG 9 is trained to break into the main passenger cabin of an aircraft in three seconds, swarming through either the emergency exits above the wings or the normal front and rear passenger doors. They came in through the emergency exits, which are designed to be crashed open in a hurry without the use of explosives.

GSG 9 made use of British stun grenades, which consist of 200 grams of explosive in a cardboard casing; there is no shrapnel, but a flash that blinds and deafens for seven seconds. Once inside the body of the aircraft the commandos used heavy hand guns and automatic rifles with a minimum of shots. There was no attempt to get the hijackers to surrender nor of shooting to wound: a wounded terrorist is highly motivated and just as likely to detonate explosives. Three were killed, one of the women wounded.

The raid took three minutes.

Within hours there were more deaths. In Stammheim prison in Germany Andreas Baader, one of the founders of the Baader-Meinhof gang whose release had been demanded by Mahmoud, used the Heckler und Koch pistol that had been smuggled into his cell to end his life. Jan-Carl Raspe also killed himself with a gun. Gudrun Ensslin used electric flex to hang herself.

The outcry was predictable. At once it was claimed that these were no suicides, they were revenge killings. In retribution, the kidnapped industrialist leader Hanns-Martin Schleyer was murdered and his body dumped in a hired car over the border near Mulhouse in France.

There were disturbing signs that, at the least, the deaths of the three terrorists in Stammheim jail were 'assisted suicides'. After all, how had the two guns found their way inside this maximum-security prison? Surely their lawyers wouldn't have gone so far as to smuggle in weapons? Surely?

And Baader had been shot from behind, apparently holding the gun in his left hand (he was left-handed) and guiding the muzzle to the back of his head with his right hand. Who ever heard of such contortions?

Finally, there was the curious question of suicide notes. There was none. Psychologically it must be impossible for a political terrorist to kill himself without leaving a defiant note.

In fact there was such a note, just one, found by the body of Ensslin, the theoretician of the terrorist group. It was suppressed not by Chancellor Helmut Schmidt nor by anyone of the prison service but by the Bundesnachrichtdienst.

The BND is the West German Intelligence Service, not normally concerned with matters of internal security. But it had become interested in the inmates of Stammheim because of the growing international nature of terrorism. Links had been discovered not just with Palestinian groups, but with Libya (which supplied much of the money) and with Iraq (international terrorist training facilities), and with organizations in Holland, Britain, Ireland, France, Japan, Norway, Uruguay, Venezuela and East Germany.

A BND officer, Klaus Biedenkopf, had been seconded to work in the prison and it was he who found the suicide letter in Ensslin's cell and removed it before the prison authorities could take charge of it. His reasoning was that the prison governor would be bound to hand it over to a political figure and it would inevitably be made public, if not at the inquest then certainly at the Ministry of Justice inquiry into the deaths. His opinion was initially rejected by superiors in the BND, who felt that any evidence of suicide was preferable to the chorus of accusation. But in the final analysis the Blood Letter, as it was coded, was suppressed on the grounds that its publication would help create a romantic myth about the dead terrorists and be an incitement to further violence. This prevailing view was put forward by Frank Duraine, a liaison officer from the CIA who was working at the BND headquarters outside Munich.

Inevitably it proved impossible to suppress all knowledge of the Blood Letter because only three out of the four succeeded in committing suicide. The fourth, Irmgard Müller, had used a bread knife and succeeded in inflicting flesh wounds on her chest that were, in the words of the Stuttgart forensic expert Professor Rauschke, "rather cautious". There were reports (unconfirmed) that when she regained consciousness in hospital she asked: *"Wo ist es? Das Blut-Brief?"* It was enough to start rumours about the Blood Letter and its contents.

Duraine secured a Xerox copy of the Blood Letter and this is filed at Agency headquarters at Langley, Virginia. It reads in translation:

> We salute our dead comrades who gave their red blood on the sands of Mogadishu in the fight against the fascist German State.
> Our blood mingles with their blood and will flow into the veins of the revolution.
> The sacrifice of our lives is our triumph.
> The fascists will not win. For each of us dead, the blood of one Western imperialist leader will be spilled.
> This letter is sealed in the red blood of us all.

The original was written in red ink. But the signatures were executed in blood, which had oxidized to a dull brown. The blood was analysed and found to be a mixture of two groups: Blood Group O (the successful suicides Baader, Ensslin and Raspe belonged to this group) and the rare AB (the still-living Müller).

Estimates of the number of hard-core terrorists in German society vary. Few put the number higher than a couple of dozen. They have a much larger group of active supporters, both in Germany and internationally, who are willing to supply money, arms, cars and safe houses.

It is in this fertile ground that the terrorist cell known as Blood Group O grew.

This will, of course, be denied.

CHAPTER ONE

The woman's scream was part of it, and the crash of splintering wood from somewhere above. Nobody had ears for that. Their voices were busy, though you couldn't tell what was being said. Their hands and eyes were restless, their bodies too tight packed to move. Fragments of sentences jutted out of the general uproar, like the worst kind of cocktail party.

And they were serving cocktails, too. In Paris, in the year 1979, they were serving cocktails.

"What's this called?" I asked.

His lips went *What?*

"What is this called?" I pointed a finger at the liquid, cloudy pink, sweetish, tasting of nothing definable.

Finally I went in close to his left ear to repeat the question and he leaned in close to give me the answer.

"I think it's the Wall Street Crash," he said. He'd informed me his name was Patrick Something. A number of Frenchmen are called Patrick, ones with high foreheads and thin cheekbones. He'd said he was Xala Xanadu's agent, but I didn't recognize the name. He'd pointed out a young woman with a lot of ebony skin, hair piled up in an ants' nest of baked clay, and white semi-circles painted under the eyes. He'd told me she was the

1

hottest property since B.B. and I'd said I was glad for her. He'd told me her latest film and I'd said I'd go and see it.

Patrick Something pecked at his glass. "Maybe it's Blues in the Night, or is that made with gin?"

"Well, what's this made of?"

"What?"

At the far end of the room there were steps leading up to a door with a peephole and chain. A man in a canary yellow shirt and a brown bowler hat inspected you through the peephole when you knocked three times; you were meant to say in English, "Joe sent us", and he would undo bolts and bars and the chain and let you in. At least, that is what it said on the invitation. I couldn't see the doorman.

There were four of them. They stood just inside the door, looking down over the room, searching someone out.

"It might even be Between the Sheets," he said.

There was a bored guy playing an old upright under a sign *Ne tirez sur le pianiste*. He sang in a thin high voice.

"We've bathtub booze
If you thirst for laughter
Scare away the blues
Till the morning after."

There were palm trees in tubs, a row of bullet holes in one wall dripping red paint, an arrow pointing vaguely upstairs with the legend *Rooms $5 an hour*.

Perhaps it had seemed like a good idea, a half century after the '29 crash, to open a night spot called *Prohibition*. I hadn't wanted to come. You can get crowds and noise and a headache on the Métro any morning, and you miss the smoke. But Desnos, who was part owner, was a friend. I'd met him four months before. We had gone to the Val d'Isère for New Year.

The four men had spotted who they wanted and were coming down the steps. The door to the cloakroom and the street had been left open and I still wondered vaguely what had happened to the doorman in his yellow shirt and brown bowler hat.

Patrick Something was explaining how to make a Ricartini. It was a dry martini with three drops of Ricard instead of a twist of lemon peel.

I said *Oh*.

A plump man with curly hair was leaning forward to peer at Xala Xanadu's left breast, which had a three-pointed pattern like knife scars from some tribal initiation ceremony. He wet a finger with saliva and rubbed at her flesh and the pattern smeared. Xala Xanadu slapped his face. Nobody paid any attention.

I hate Paris when it tries to impress itself. Brittle, unheeding, irrelevant. I looked for Desnos, to tell him I was leaving, and caught sight of the four men again, a pool of leather at the bottom of the steps, the last of them to descend wearing dark glasses and a denim cap.

There weren't more than two or three people I knew in the room; the rest were the sort who get invited to the opening night of a new club and come because the booze is free. They were film people, PR people, people in real estate in Ibiza, smooth young men from Havas Conseil, the daughters of industrialists. Someone said Françoise Sagan had been invited.

"No," Patrick Something said, turning from a waiter in apron and striped jerkin and concertina metal sleevebands. "Apparently it's called a Bathtub Bang."

I moved away from Patrick Something. He made to follow and a sluggish tide of people came between us.

It was the leather jackets. They had snagged in my mind. The leather jackets and the scream.

Most of the men wore suits with wide shoulders and broad lapels and kept on their big-brimmed hats as if it were fancy dress. There were women in cloche hats and strings of beads and peekaboo eyes. The model girls with flat chests looked authentic in V-necked dresses.

Still no sign of the doorman and I wondered if the scream I'd picked up had been the hat-check girl, and the crash the doorman knocking over her table.

Next to me a man in a velvet bow tie made a speech to no one in particular, deserted by his audience. His head was tipped back and he gestured with a finger. " … transposing *Boule de Suif* to the Seinan War period so that not only is the violence exquisite … "

It began at that moment. I heard a shout above the uproar. Beside me the voice droned on.

" … but he does manage to evoke the political and moral ambiguities of the Japan of 1878 … "

Everyone in that first-night crowd was convinced it was a "happening", part of the fun, a staged raid on a speakeasy. People turned towards the excitement and as a gap opened up I saw the four men who'd come in leather jackets and they all wore dark glasses now. I counted three guns. The fourth man had his back turned, speaking to someone I couldn't see.

Perhaps a quarter of the guests were watching the little tableau and there was still a high level of noise. But I could hear a woman's high-pitched voice quite distinctly, *"Ah, c'est sensass,"* and I saw her lean forward to kiss the cheek of one of the men in leather jacket and dark glasses and holding an automatic pistol.

She got his hand in her chest and went quite a long way back into the crowd, and it was her shriek that made a lot more people turn and crane their necks.

A man near me stood on tiptoe and said to his companion: "Gilles is clever, putting on a show like this." Gilles was Desnos, the part owner, my friend.

And then I moved away to stand at the edge of the room.

I wanted to have my back to the wall because I didn't know whether there might be more men with guns in their hands that I hadn't noticed. I braced one foot against the wall so that if I had to move it would give me impetus to push into the crowd.

There were more shouts across the room and a man swung a punch, one of those long-telegraphed, wild punches people learn from TV Westerns.

But it wasn't part of the cabaret. I knew they wouldn't come in leather jackets and jeans if they were the floorshow. They'd have dressed in baggy pants and neck-scarves, worn hats with snapped-down brims, and carried violin cases. They'd have kept it *rétro*.

There was no nostalgia about these men.

The shot was quite loud in the low-ceilinged room, attracting the attention of the rest of the guests. People at the back were pressing forward. Even those at the front weren't anxious, merely curious.

The whiteness of a face caught my eye and it was Patrick Something. He was grinning, sharing his appreciation of the fun.

The four men in leather jackets pushed back through the crowd towards the steps. The last of the four moved backwards, clutching his gun, watching faces and hands.

A male voice shrilled: "Marvellous, my dears. I'll get Louis to put you in the next production."

On the floor a body lay stretched out. All I could see were the legs from the knees down, with grotesque purple suede shoes pointing their toes to heaven.

"Look, *tomato ketchup*," a woman said, using the English words. She giggled. "Chabrol told me about *tomato ketchup*. Under the shirt they have this plastic bag…"

The shrill man interrupted: "Oh please, not Chabrol…"

They didn't run up the steps. Their movements were deliberate, economical, knowing what had to be done. Only the last man showed any tension. At the top the first three vanished through the open door; the last man looked all round, his mouth open, stuffed the pistol into his pocket, ran out into the night.

A deep voice shouted, "Cut." There was a little laughter.

A woman said: 'That was sensational, Gilles," and the crowd turned back from watching the exit.

"Gilles?"

A glass shattered on the floor.

I could hear a low sobbing, a girl's, from up above in the cloakroom.

Some of the people who'd had ringside seats by the action were kneeling near the body on the floor. One man got to his feet, his tanned face paling even in these lights, a hand covering his mouth, staring at the red on the fingers of his other hand.

The pianist had never stopped playing. Something by Scott Joplin now.

Somebody said, *"Bon Dieu,"* not very loudly.

Over and over the woman's voice said, "Gilles? ... Gilles? ... Gilles? ... "

My friend Gilles Desnos had grotesque taste in shoes. I suddenly remembered that.

CHAPTER TWO

He was dead. That was my first thought.

I saw his narrow body and cramped face in the wedge of light from the door. He was in the straight-backed chair, tilted against the wall by the desk, a slack heap of bones and clothes. He stared and stared with that stillness which is final. Then I saw the glint of his eyeballs go off and on as he blinked and I came into my apartment, shutting the door to the stairs.

No greeting.

I turned on the light in the living room and checked the bedroom, the bathroom, the kitchen. He'd come alone. When I went back into the living room he hadn't moved. His eyes were on me.

I thought: You've come for your gun. There was something about the expression in his eyes. They weren't the narrow eyes that threaten; they were round eyes that knew something I didn't. There was coldness in them too; but as the years mount, all police show that. And the ones whose patch is security have eyes so cold they've lost all colour.

Because it was Crevecoeur I knew he'd wait for me to make the first move. Some do it because they're alert for twitches and guilty knowledge. With Crevecoeur it was a game: he liked to watch you work it all out; he liked to feel superior.

I went back into the hall, looking in the closet, but it wasn't there. I found it thrown across a chair, the same old fawn raincoat with a twisted belt and dirty collar. The cloth was dry though it was one of those squally March nights that throw the rain in your face. His face was dry too.

I sat on a chair facing him and held up three fingers of my right hand and bent them over as I spoke.

"One: your coat's dry so you've been here long enough to make a thorough search. Two: if I asked you, you would say it was to recover your gun; but I told you it would be kept in a secure place. Really it was opportunism; you wouldn't miss a chance on your own to spy. Three: my *carte de séjour* was renewed last month and if you're here now it's because you expect some pay-off."

His hand moved.

"And that's all, Cody?"

All? I could have made a dozen petty deductions. He'd sat in the dark while he waited, so he wanted to surprise me. He hadn't smoked, because I'd smell that when I opened the door. Mme Boyer had let him past her concierge's window but not warned me, so she spied for him. On and on.

He was probing, trying to turn up my shabby little secrets. I said: "No woman should tell a man everything."

Crevecoeur smiled. It was the only chink I'd found in his professional armour: he rose to a sexual innuendo.

"I suppose you'd like coffee," I said.

He sighed. "Whisky would be nice."

I went into the kitchen and began the business with the kettle and the coffee-grinder and the drip-filters. Coffee would take away the taste of Blues in the Night or whatever it had been at the *Prohibition*, that cloudy liquid in the glass, the four men in leather jackets, the sound of the shot.

I blocked the memory. Not now, because of Crevecoeur. He'd followed into the kitchen to watch. He'd be leaning against the wall behind me, blinking because the kitchen light was harsher and his eyes were rimmed with fatigue. I didn't have to look. I heard his sigh again, the body's attempt to draw in extra oxygen.

"It's been a difficult day?" I was a cretin; it was no business of mine if his day had been hard. Crevecoeur was working to create the domestic atmosphere and that's the trouble with his kind: let them in just once and they stake a claim to a part of your life and believe they can unlock your apartment door whenever they want their hand held.

I live in the half world. Half in the light of day, half in the shadows. So, in his way, did Crevecoeur. But his position was recognized by the French State, blessed with the approval of the bureaucrats. Whereas I didn't exist, didn't have an official existence; let one of the grey men with their rubber stamps find out some of the things I had done and I would be on the first plane west across the Atlantic.

But in my half world I lived my own life, made my own decisions, my own friends, my own enemies.

Crevecoeur was no friend of mine. He could even be an enemy. He was a Chief Inspector in the Sûreté Nationale—should be higher now if President Giscard had shown any political gratitude. I only knew him because I had been caught up in Cold War games and I'd had to run very hard to keep alive. The first attempt on my life, five months ago, had followed directly on Crevecoeur's first visit to my apartment. There had been half a dozen of them waiting for me in the dark and one had been armed with an automatic rifle. Someone must have made a phone call to Extension 48 at the Soviet embassy and I was ninety-nine per cent certain it had been Crevecoeur.

"Bloody difficult," he replied. I'd forgotten what my question was.

Because I lived in the half world, I had to accept Crevecoeur. The game has no written rules, there is no referee to blow the whistle on foul play, and if there are any spectators, they never cheer.

"It's a game we play, isn't it?" he remarked. I looked up at him sharply because I hadn't spoken out loud. "Who was it said that spying was the great game?"

"A writer," I told him, "not a doer."

He smiled again, lips tight across his teeth. His face was thin, with vertical creases as if it had been slammed in a door once. He held his head on one side, sparrow-like, while I poured boiling water into the filters.

Crevecoeur could be right. It was a game we played, like the power game between East and West, each side with its underground ICBM silos and a finger poised over the red button. I had his gun, the one that had killed the French reporter Pasquier in East Berlin; he had the power to revoke my residence permit and drop the tax man on my head. But neither was a "viable first-strike weapon", as the generals would have it; because each invited unacceptable retaliation.

"It's a game, Cody," he repeated. "A game like chess. We know chess isn't life. But once one gets involved, one wants to win the game. No, not wants, *has* to win, a compulsion. Let's go back to the living room."

I checked my watch as we went and it said well after midnight. I was tired. Any day in which you witness a friend's murder is tiring.

I mustn't think of that.

Crevecoeur caught the glance at my watch and said: "I don't want to keep you. You look exhausted."

He made me angry. He always had. He angered me with his deceptions, his assumption he could break into your life, telling you what you should do, telling you that your face was stained with shock and sadness.

"I've been to a terrible party." The cliché, for once, was true.

"Yes," he said. "Your friend Desnos."

The anger clenched tight in my chest. He was a sharp-nosed dog, always sniffing at lamp posts.

He couldn't have heard already about what had happened at the *Prohibition*. I had walked straight up the steps, past the bruised doorman and wailing hat-check girl, out into the rain before the police had even been sent for. I'd run down to the river and along the *quai,* a blind, blundering run because I desperately wanted to take some action, snagging against people's shoulders, looking for them, looking for the four men with leather jackets and professional cool. There was the hiss of tyres on wet tarmac and a woman's laughter. Nothing else. In any case if they'd come by car it would have been stolen or have had false plates. They wouldn't make elementary errors. Nothing I could do. I turned back to rue Saint-André-des-Arts, climbed the stairs to my apartment. An hour ago Desnos had been alive.

I had to block out the memory again.

Crevecoeur positioned himself again in the straight-backed chair. It was easy to see the attraction of it for him. The wooden chair, the desk, the telephone, gave him the reassurance of his own office; he was the boss, nothing threatened his authority.

I asked: "Why have you come?"

The coffee was still hot and he drank it in small sips, holding the cup in both hands, peering at me over the rim and down again.

"Let me be perfectly frank." It was a bad beginning and he knew it and stopped, frowning. "Cody, it's like this. I want you to do something and I know you don't want to do it and so it's difficult for me. You don't want to do it because of what I am and what happened in the past and maybe because you simply don't like me. But you mustn't let what happened a few months ago sour your judgement."

What had happened a few months ago was that he had attempted to trade me in to the MfS in East Berlin. That didn't cloud my judgement; it made it crystal clear.

He went on: "You're twenty-eight, I think?"

"Yes."

"Never married?"

"No."

"But there have been liaisons along the way. I mean serious involvements. Dolbiac I met briefly, someone in the State Department called Martin, a man ... "

"It's not your concern."

"Pardon me if I seem inquisitive. But it is my concern. It's my job to know things." He drank another sip of coffee. He insisted: "But no children?"

His kind are always happiest asking questions. The more they know, the more they can control. It is the only thing they believe in.

I folded my arms.

He said: "There are some women who don't like children and I suppose the world would condemn them as unnatural. You're not like that. You have no children because how could you, the life you lead. But you like kids, you even took the Duhamel boy to the circus at Christmas."

He paused. I suppose my look must have been sharp on his face. He had been knocking on doors, asking questions, watching; and I'd suspected nothing. I was growing careless.

He said: "You have no children of your own but you like them. You can understand what a mother and father feel about a child, the love, the desire to protect, the anguish when something goes wrong."

It was late and I'd had enough of the soap opera, of the sound of violins. "Come to the point."

"One last question: do you know a man called Poelsma?"

I gave it three seconds. Poelsma wasn't a friend or acquaintance. The name was uncommon and maybe I'd heard or read about it but the feeling was too vague to pursue.

"No."

"All right, I'll tell you about Theo Poelsma. He is a diamond broker, Dutch by birth, thiry-nine last birthday, lives mainly in

Paris, has a French wife, Justine. They tell me the wife is beautiful and is gratified when a man tells her so, but I have no personal knowledge of that."

What the woman did was no concern of his, no more than my relationships were. He was a voyeur, thirsty for secret knowledge.

"Poelsma's family has had a traditional connection with the diamond trade and the business he has built up means he is a moderately rich man. By moderately rich I mean enough money to have a house in Paris, a second in the Var, and a third in Amsterdam. They have one child, Simone, aged nine. Being an only child she is the centre of much attention. Being the only child of rich parents, Simone provides a special temptation to others. It's an industry in Italy; it's growing in France."

It was raining again. Crevecoeur kept pausing because he knew the imagination must be allowed time to work, and in the break I heard the wind throwing the rain at the window. The drops tap-tapped like small fingers at the pane of glass.

And that was why he'd come? Waited for me until midnight? I was no Philip Marlowe tracking down poor little rich girls. He hadn't said it in so many words so I asked: "You mean the daughter Simone has been kidnapped?"

"Correct."

There was another of his little pauses. He tipped the cup and drained the last of his coffee. He was giving me the opportunity to become interested, but he was wasting his time. I wouldn't play. But I asked anyway: "Why haven't I seen any newspaper headlines?"

"Because Poelsma hasn't reported Simone missing to the *police judiciaire*. Kidnappers always insist: no police. It seldom works out like that because there's usually someone hurt or there are witnesses. However this time there was nobody wounded and there were no outside witnesses. Poelsma didn't telephone the local police, he came to the Sûreté Nationale, which was absolutely right, because kidnapping is becoming a national threat to society and the gangs must be crushed. It's not only the children of the rich who are snatched. If the father works in a position of responsibility in a big corporation, preferably multi-national or American-owned because that is politically more acceptable, that corporation can be blackmailed into paying for the return of the child."

"If it's the Sûreté's job, you do something about it. You can't go knocking on doors saying, 'Hey, you like kids, go get this one back for us.' "

"Ah," he said.

He got out his packet of Gitanes and lit one. A cloud of grey drifted towards the ceiling and he stared into it, seeing something, concentrating, his face squeezed tight as an accordion. Then he stretched out a hand and opened a drawer in my desk and fiddled for something. Let him. He'd long ago have sifted through the concert notes and Air France timetables and dead letters.

"There are two reasons why I can do nothing about Poelsma," he said. "First, you know the nature of the Sûreté Nationale because it is notorious, little better than SDECE. It is like a sieve, riddled with double agents and informers, leaking secrets everywhere. Some of the secrets drip on Moscow, some on Peking, some on Washington. Then there are connections with the criminal milieu. If I start asking questions, the kidnappers will hear at once. If I plan a move, they will be one jump ahead. You know that to be true because you have had experience of it. I would have reporters and TV cameras following my car, photographers from *Paris-Match* asking me to hold up my handcuffs and look stern." He found a paperclip in the drawer and destroyed it. "Perhaps you think I should take a fortnight's vacation and work on it away from rue des Saussaies. I do not have the time. That is the second reason I can do nothing. On Sunday the *Sommet* begins. I have been placed in charge of security for the President and there is simply no time for other matters."

It was the evergreen problem of the Middle East. There had been conferences in Geneva and Cairo and Tel Aviv. Now there was going to be a Summit in Amsterdam with Israel, Egypt, America, Britain, West Germany and France sitting round the table and talking for the electorate back home.

The press had been full of nothing else. You didn't have to buy a newspaper to know about it, you could read the headlines from fifty metres down the street. "Will Israel yield?" "US pressure for a settlement." "My hopes for peace", by somebody or other. What did it matter—they hadn't invited the Palestinians. What did it matter if they did ask the Palestinians—there would always be a hard core who rejected any kind of peace.

It was silent in the room except for the noise like a clock ticking. I have no clock. It was the rain dripping on the sill from the cracked guttering above.

So the fate of a kidnapped nine-year-old girl was nothing compared with the safety of a president. Did Crevecoeur expect me to show anger or surprise at that?

"No," I told him. "The kidnapped girl is your problem, the leaks in the SN are your problem, security at the Summit is also your problem. None of it is to do with me. I will not do a job for you. You know that."

He didn't know that.

He got up and did a slow tour of the room. He stopped by the bookcase and considered the Klymchuk painting on the wall above, his head on one side. It was typical of Klymchuk in his early style: you couldn't tell whether he was being surreal or erotic or making a social comment. The canvas showed a nude girl sprawled across a tousled bed, one foot lifted to rest on the wall; a shadow lay across her body so that it seemed she was half black, half white; the man who stood over her wore uniform and a high-peaked military cap and had a duelling scar down his cheek; he stared at the girl's naked body but what upset people was there were no eyes in his face.

"Strangely," Crevecoeur said, "I'm confident you are going to help me. I'll let you think about it."

Suddenly I was fully alert. That was it? No more? No pressure, no pleas? It was out of character for him to drop it and you should always be frightened when a cop acts out of character.

I noticed the rain gusting at the window again and so did Crevecoeur. He went and put on his coat. He was tying the belt slowly when he spoke again.

"By the way, I had lunch with an old, mmm, friend of yours. You haven't forgotten Duraine, have you?" I didn't reply and he went on fiddling with the belt. "He was passing through on his way to Amsterdam. He's also caught up in the security arrangements for the conference. He said if I saw you again I should pass on his, mmm, regards."

I hadn't forgotten Duraine. I'd run against him first in Berlin. He'd tricked me into doing some business in Turkey. And now he'd had lunch with Crevecoeur. Duraine worked for the Agency, as I once had, and it seemed I could never be rid of him.

"You knew McKosker too, didn't you?" Crevecoeur went on. His tone was casual, just repeating gossip, just rubbing in I was somebody with a past. "He was getting quite high in the structure at Langley but apparently he was pushed out in Stansfield Turner's great purge. Duraine maintained the atmosphere at the Agency was almost as bad as at the KGB during one of Beria's purges. But Duraine himself seems to be doing well."

Duraine would always do well. He was this kind of man: if you shook hands with him, you should count your fingers afterwards.

I stood up. I was too angry to say anything: the thought of Duraine and Crevecoeur discussing me, my affairs, my life.

Crevecoeur came and stood very close in front of me. I could smell the Gitane on his breath. He looked for something in my face and nodded.

He was gone.

I watched him through the gap between the curtains as he came out on to the sidewalk below, hunching his shoulders against the night. He looked left and right, crossed the street and set off in the direction of boulevard Saint-Michel. As he passed under the street lamp, the rain formed a halo round his head. It was only a trick of the light.

Afterwards, long afterwards when it was all over, I wondered if it was Crevecoeur's intention right from the start that I should be killed. On balance I think not.

It's just that when I was minutes away from death he made no effort to save me.

CHAPTER THREE

Within twenty-four hours Crevecoeur had hooked me.

The bell was insistent. Some part of my brain said it was Debbie riding round the neighbour's lawn ringing her bicycle bell and then it was an intruder alarm and then it was a mad winning streak on one of Gottlieb's pinball wonders and then it was the telephone.

"Hallo."

"I'm sorry to wake you."

I looked at my watch and it showed exactly eight o'clock, as if he'd been waiting for the bureaucratically approved hour to needle me. I must have made a noise.

Crevecoeur said: "I'm flying to Amsterdam to see the security people there about the Middle East conference and I'll be back late this evening, so you can see there's no way I can deal with Poelsma's missing girl today."

I made the mistake of treating him as human. I should have replaced the receiver without involving myself. Instead I tried reason: "You probably have one hundred and fifty people at your level or above at the Sûreté. Hand it over to one of them."

"Cody, you amaze me. Is there a single person working here you'd trust?"

My brain fought for an answer. I hadn't taken Seconal but it had been very late before I could sleep. After Crevecoeur had left, thoughts of Gilles had crowded in.

"I have arranged for you to meet someone," he began, and he continued forcibly when I tried to interrupt. "Don't protest. There is a little girl who is alive but may not be for much longer and I'm asking you to help. You'd run to help her if she was in a car crash and this is no different. Except we have a chance to prevent it."

I felt the clenched fist of anger in my belly and I told him he was a blackmailing shit.

"Yes. Now you have time for coffee and then at nine o'clock be at Notre-Dame. Dress like a tourist. Carry a copy of the *Herald-Tribune* and the Fodor guide. Sit in the aisle seat, on the left, ten rows from the entrance."

He'd been reading *Le Dossier Ipcress* again.

"Why do we have to play these games?"

"So she'll recognize you."

"She?"

"The little girl's nanny."

"Oh Jesus, Crevecoeur, a nanny."

"Listen to what she has to say. I'll be in touch when I get back from Holland."

"What's the verbal code-intro for March—Christopher Robin is Saying His Prayers?"

But he'd been waiting for the flip tone of voice: no more protests. There was an eerie whistling noise in my ear.

I sat in the aisle seat, on the left side, ten rows from the entrance.

If Crevecoeur had a watchman in Notre-Dame I couldn't pick him out. He could easily have attached himself to one of the groups. It wasn't the full flood of the tourist season but Paris is never free of them. They moved slowly, shepherded by girls with badges: Vingresor, American Express, Voyages Havas.

"This is where Napoleon crowned himself emperor."

"That is the Last Judgement above the portal."

"These are representations of Heaven and Hell."

You could pick her out from the way she walked, let alone the way she dressed. She held herself erect, her neck straight, her hands clasped in front of her, looking directly ahead. She wore a dark blue coat, buttoned and belted, dark blue hat with a white cloth flower, dark blue shoes, dark blue bag over her arm. She paused while her eyes took in my newspaper and guidebook and then she was in the pew.

"On your knees," she said.

"I beg your pardon?"

"On your knees," she said. "This is a house of God."

She knelt and turned grey eyes to scrutinize me. "I take it you are not a heathen."

I knelt beside her and rested my chin on my hands.

"Almighty God, who alone has the power to right the evils of this world, we beseech you to return to safety this little innocent, Simone. We pray that she comes to no further harm and that her experience will be of lasting benefit in instructing her in the wicked ways of man. And if it be your desire, Lord, we urge you in your mercy to smite the sinners."

The voice was clear and precise. She was from Scotland. I think I can distinguish a Glasgow accent but no more. She was not Glaswegian.

"Amen," she concluded. She'd been waiting for me to say it.

I moved to sit back on the bench and she put out a restraining hand.

"Stay. I am accustomed to praying in church and I have a notion it would do you no harm to be on your knees. You are the young woman whom Chief Inspector Crevecoeur instructed me to see?"

She pronounced the last syllable of his name *cur*, rolling the "r".

"Yes."

"He instructed me to inform you of all the relevant details of this tragedy and answer any of your queries. He seemed to have faith you would be able to help restore the girl to her family."

"It is not really my business ... "

"I have been the girl's nanny for two years." She spoke in the firm tone of someone who did not expect to be interrupted. "Please God she shall be returned unharmed and then I shall be away home. Enough is enough. My sister keeps a private hotel in Edinburgh and I'm thinking business will be improving there and she'll have need of some assistance. In any case the child is too old for a nanny and I have no desire to stay with these folk any longer."

"You're referring to the parents?"

"Aye, indeed I am. You are not acquainted with them?"

"Not at all."

"It is not my practice to gossip, especially in a house of God, but the Lord knows all secrets and will know this is the truth. The last nanny they had for the girl was what I am informed the English call a dolly-bird. She left when it could no longer be concealed she was with child. It was Madame Poelsma who conducted the interviews for a successor: no female under the age of fifty was considered."

We looked at each other and she nodded briefly.

"Enough said."

"Tell me how Simone was kidnapped."

"I can give you precious little in the way of detail. It happened three days ago. I was attending church—not, you understand, a Catholic temple such as this, but the British embassy church in rue d'Aguesseau. Matins, every Sunday morning, ten-thirty. Monsieur and Madame Poelsma had no religion. If they had taken Simone to church, this would never have occurred. Mark that: God makes his purpose known in diverse ways. When I returned to the house about a quarter to twelve or a little later, it was to a scene one normally associates with television melodramas. The maid was having hysterics and the cook had stopped preparations for Sunday lunch. I could get no sense from them.

"I have my own quarters on the second floor but I went first to the drawing room to see if Simone was there. Although she does not attend church, no charge of mine is brought up an ignorant savage, and on Sunday mornings she reads the scriptures with me for half an hour before lunch.

"I'm sure I do not need to impress on you that I am not in the habit of eavesdropping. But Madame Poelsma's voice was raised and there was no way of avoiding it as I crossed the hall. She was saying, screaming might be a more accurate description, 'Answer me, if you've never met her, why did she call you *Theo*? Tell me the reason. Why did she say, *Surprise, surprise, Theo*? Was she another of your—', and she used a particular expression."

"Madame Poelsma was speaking French?"

"It is a tongue I am perfectly well acquainted with. I knocked and entered. Monsieur held a glass, of whisky or brandy I have no doubt, and there was a certain amount of blood from a gash near the hairline by his left temple. Madame was on the sofa, crouching on all fours, like a spitting she-cat. The scene impressed itself on me. I said, 'Pardon, madame, I was looking for Simone.' She replied, 'She's gone, stolen, abducted. Ask him. He knows about it.' Monsieur seemed to be in shock, not even drinking his whisky, and since Madame offered no further explanations I returned to the kitchen.

"Half an hour previously Janine the maid, and a flighty girl, had answered the front doorbell and a girl and two young fellows were outside. Janine was confused in her memory but she thought both the young men wore their hair long and one had a blond beard. The girl said: 'We've come to see Theo Poelsma. He's expecting us.' They pushed through without so much as a by-your-leave. Janine was returning to the kitchen where she was helping with the vegetables when she heard a shout of some kind, a scream from Madame, and shrieks from the wee girl. By the time Janine had collected her wits and run back upstairs, the front door was gaping wide and the bairn gone. That, as I say, was on Sunday morning."

"You yourself didn't actually witness anything?"

Her mouth was tight with disapproval before she answered. "Except for the conduct of Madame and Monsieur, and the behaviour of the domestics." And then she looked down the aisle at approaching figures.

"It is the will of God, *maman*, it is part of God's plan, *maman*, it is the will of God, *maman*, we must not question his wisdom *maman*."

The daughter's voice was like a soft chant. She had an arm round her mother's shoulders as they progressed away from the transept.

"He was in the prime of life, the finest man on earth, he was a rock."

"It is the will of God, *maman*."

The mother was in black: her dress, her veil, her life.

The Scots woman watched them pass and turned back to me. Her expression was unbending: if it was God's great design, you should not weep.

"What is your name?" It hadn't occurred to me to ask. She had just been a creation of Crevecoeur's.

"Tulloch," she answered. "Miss Tulloch, that is."

Of course.

I have known a lot of people in what is loosely called "the Intelligence community" and there is no common type. They can be violent, subtle, ambitious, emotional, organizational, imaginative, devious. Crevecoeur was the cleverest. He knew when to ask questions and when not. He knew when to give the information, he knew the sort of details that hooked into the imagination. He knew when to leave you alone. He knew I would accept the abduction of Simone when told by Miss Tulloch but not by him.

"That is not the end of the matter," she said. "There were no regular police in uniforms but this security man Crevecoeur interviewed us all separately. Did we recognize anybody? Had we noticed anybody suspicious lurking outside? I imagine that is all routine. That was Sunday afternoon. On Monday morning I rose as usual at six-thirty and went downstairs—I have no facilities for making tea in my quarters though I have spoken more than once to Madame Poelsma about it. On the hall floor by the front door there was a package, a brown manila envelope. It struck me as odd because it was too early for the postal delivery. I picked the envelope up. I am not, I need hardly stress, in the habit of reading others' mail but there was no addressee's name on the envelope and the flap was unsealed. I looked inside and there was hair, a considerable quantity of hair, dark, in ringlets, about a foot in length. I recognized it at once. It was the same texture and shade and even smell as Simone's. There was also a single sheet of white typing paper and it had written on it in capital letters: *NO POLICE. WE EXPECT YOU TO CO-OPERATE. IF NOT, THE EARS NEXT TIME.*"

That was what they'd done to Paul Getty's grandson in Rome. The ear had come through the post as an encouragement. With Baron Empain it had been a fingertip.

"Those were the exact words?" It puzzled me.

"I have always prided myself on the fidelity of my memory. The words were written in English with a soft pencil."

"There was nothing else?"

"Nothing."

"What did you do?"

"I replaced the hair and note in the envelope, put it on the floor, returned to my room and … "

"You didn't take the letter to show the Poelsmas?"

"I went down on my knees and prayed for forgiveness for reading someone else's private communication and for the safety of the child. To what purpose should I have woken Madame and Monsieur? What good news did the letter convey? Monsieur Poelsma saw it before breakfast in any case."

"What did he do?"

"Nothing. He remained in the house all day. There was nothing for me to do. I wrote a letter to my sister and waited. We all waited."

"There were no police outside?"

"There was nobody."

She couldn't be certain. She'd have no experience of sensing-out discreet surveillance. A closed van, an upstairs window, a street-sweeper.

"Crevecoeur didn't come?"

"No."

I was going to question her because the whole set-up seemed crazy but she looked quite certain.

"Do you know if Poelsma telephoned him?"

"I think I have said I am not in the habit of eavesdropping."

"So you wouldn't know when the kidnappers got in touch again?"

"Ah, to the best of my knowledge, they didn't. Monsieur had withdrawn to his study, Madame sent for me to keep her company in the drawing room. You can hear the telephone perfectly from there. It rang from Monsieur's office in the morning and he told them he didn't want to be disturbed with business. Otherwise, a few social calls, which it was not my intention to hear, as I have said."

"Yes, you told me." She would be perfect as a concierge. There would be no ungodly levity at her sister's private hotel in Edinburgh.

"Towards six in the evening Monsieur came out from the study, holding his briefcase, and announced he was leaving. Madame asked where he was going, and he made me leave the room before answering."

"You didn't hear, by chance … "

I sensed the stiffness in her body and left it.

I walked out from Notre-Dame into place du Parvis, my knees stiff from kneeling. Miss Tulloch had added nothing more of importance. She prayed God would guide me to recover the little girl. There were no tears on her face. I wondered if there had ever been a smile.

The sun was shining and puffball clouds gambolled across the blue. I walked to the pont au Double and stared down at the river. It was the contradictions that puzzled me.

There are two sorts of kidnapping: straight criminal and political.

In criminal, the gang keeps a low profile and makes private contact with the family or business group and puts forward its demands: a million dollars and don't bring the police.

In political, the gang at the very outset makes a loud public statement: we have struck this blow against the wicked imperialists and in the name of the revolution. Then come the demands: money and the release of prisoners.

This was neither.

No money was mentioned in the note, there had been no further communication, nobody had rung up AFP to get publicity in the press, Poelsma hadn't told Crevecoeur about the hair and letter.

It didn't make sense.

I stopped. I was thinking about it as Crevecoeur knew I would and I had to stop. A thousand tragedies happen in Paris every day and it is the business of friends and family to help and comfort. If the need for action is there, then it is the business of the police.

This was for Crevecoeur, or for someone from his department.

I had my own little tragedy to worry about: the murder of my friend.

CHAPTER FOUR

He was, I had been told, the second most powerful man in Paris.

It had been one of those relentless parties that Gilles Desnos liked to go to. The party could have been given by Alain Delon or Peyrefitte or any one of a dozen of the types who'd been at the *Prohibition*. Desnos had taken me to a succession of such affairs where the drinks, the faces, the voices, the conceit and the vanity had all been the same.

"Do you see that guy over there, the big one?" The man who had asked the question had been a little man with a widow's peak of chestnut hair and buttons for eyes. "He is the second most powerful man in Paris."

"What's his name?"

"Fonza."

I'd watched Fonza standing very still while people came to speak to him. One at a time they approached and had their say and he'd stood immobile, the second most powerful man in Paris, listening, occasionally interrupting with a question. He was a king granting an audience, dismissing supplicants with a slight nod or shake of his head. Only men came to speak to him; women who tried to catch his eye were ignored. When he left the room, there were dark stocky men in front and behind.

"They're *Corsicos*," the widow's peak had told me, leaning forward as if it were a secret.

Fonza's house was in the Sixteenth, the same arrondissement that Poelsma lived in. It was a short street of solid buildings put up at the turn of the century. Two of the more imposing had short gravel drives that curved in and out in a semi-circle. Fonza's house was one of them. There were stone pineapples on the gateposts, a line of evergreens with dark glossy leaves, and a cluster of floodlights on a tall metal pole. A man in a charcoal uniform admired his face in the chrome of a Peugeot 604.

I'd wanted to stop and study the house before I committed myself, but two men sat in a car parked at the kerb opposite the gates, watching me come closer. I should have had a story-line. I should have had a dog on a lead, a poodle that sniffed at tree-trunks, and then I'd have had good reason to stop and wait. I turned right between the gateposts and glimpsed one of the men in the car speaking into a hand-held mike. They still stared.

I pushed the button by the door. It was the sort of house where an unheard bell rang in the depths and you waited for the maid to come.

The door opened the width of two eyes and they weren't the maid's.

"Yes?"

"I want to see Monsieur Fonza."

"He sent for you?"

"No."

"You a *poule*?"

"No."

"What do you want?"

"To see Fonza."

He blinked and shut the door, but it was only to unhook the chain.

"Come in."

He was small, dark, with a Browning automatic in his hand.

"Turn round and put your hands on the wall. Come on, move."

He patted down my sides and legs. Another man stood by the stairs at the end of the hall, his arms folded.

"All right, your bag."

He searched, picked out the *carte de séjour.*

"You're British? Your name's Cody?"

"Yes."

"Why do you want to see the *capo*?"

"That concerns him and me."

"Merde."

I got his left hand across my cheek and I could feel the hotness as the blood came into the bruised area.

The man by the stairs opened his mouth and a plump tongue like a pink mouse came out and took the air and disappeared.

"I met Fonza at a private party. He said I should see him if people got tough with me. He gave me this address. He's at home because his car is outside. So let's go and see him before you make any more stupid mistakes. Fonza doesn't appreciate kids who make mistakes."

The lies came easily. I had simply rung a friend in the "morgue" at *France-Soir* for Fonza's address.

The little man didn't like me. I stared at him and his eyes shrouded with uncertainty. He said something in Corsican dialect to the man by the stairs, and to me, "Don't try any stunts", and disappeared up above.

The second man eased away from the stairs and jerked his right arm. The knife slipped out of the sleeve into his hand. The trick would have meant a lot of rehearsal, a lot of pain, before he'd got the action so smooth that the blade no longer drew blood. He stood still a moment so I would register the knife and then he threw.

The length of the hall was nearly twenty metres and at that distance it would be a triple-spin. The blade made a solid noise as it lodged in the walnut of the front door. I looked and it was still quivering in the exact centre of the panelling. The knife was lightweight, not much shock stopping power, but he had accuracy. He'd be the sort who spent an hour a day practising with an envelope pinned to a tree; then he'd go after thrushes and blackbirds; then hares; then deer. Then he'd be ready for people.

He took quick steps to retrieve the knife, slipped it out of sight. His tongue reappeared; it didn't lick his lips, it simply came out as if the need was urgent to release some pressure.

We kept silence until the first man returned.

"Come on."

Fonza sat at a heavy desk with two external phones, an internal squawkbox, an ashtray with crushed half-smoked cigarettes. He was big without looking a thug. He had a big face too, with a lipline moustache and eyes that didn't blink as I walked from the door of his office to the client's chair in front of the desk. Nothing would make those eyes uneasy, no matter what they witnessed.

He flipped down the switch on the squawkbox. "No calls." And then to me: "Pietri says you are English and called Cody. Well, *lady*," he used the English word, "I don't know your name, I have never done business with you, I have never laid eyes on you. Explain yourself."

"I lied so I would get to see you."

The man who'd brought me upstairs stirred, restless at the idea I had made him a fool. Fonza stared some more then picked a cigarette out of a pack of Bastos and lit it. The smoke flared through his nostrils like an old painting of a dragon.

"You make it sound very simple, *lady*. If a man had pulled that little trick, I'd have had Pietri on the streets again. Because you are a woman, he was not so careful. He'll learn before he grows much older. Tell me why you are here."

"A man pointed you out to me once and said you were one of the two most powerful men in Paris."

"One moment. Who told you this?"

"I don't know his name."

"Nobody forgets names. A man who forgets names never knows who his enemies are."

"I didn't say I'd forgotten. I said I didn't know."

He drew on the cigarette and looked and looked.

"All right, *lady*, a man you don't know told you I was one of the two most important men in Paris. You have walked past a half dozen of my staff and now you are sitting in that chair. Why?"

There are times we do something extremely foolish and feel no fear. This wasn't one of them.

I said: "At eleven o'clock last night a friend of mine was killed. Four men walked into his club, it was an opening-night party, shot him dead and walked out again. It was a very public murder and that's usually meant as a warning to others. A warning to me for being his friend? A warning to other club owners not to fall behind with their payments? I want to know who the men were who walked into the club last night. Were they yours?"

There was one of those silences in the room when you notice very small sounds. The man called Pietri was somewhere over towards the window behind me and I heard the rustle of his jacket as he moved an arm. On the same floor, a room or two away, there came the tapping of a manual typewriter. The chauffeur outside whistled "Yesterday". Fonza crushed a cigarette and it made a sound like a footfall in sand.

"There are a number of possibilities, *lady*. You could be very foolish, or very brave, or very ignorant. You could be trying to provoke an interesting situation on somebody else's part. You could be lying for a reason I cannot guess." His wide-set eyes ranged round my face. "British, right? Maybe you represent somebody from the United States?"

"No."

"No one with territorial ambitions? I heard Alessandro flew in from Chicago."

"I have no connections with anybody." Perhaps I should have told him but I didn't. Yes, I was British and I was recruited by the spies. It was a bad time for SIS, with Soviet moles discovered and the Americans wary of working with the Brits. Someone in the Secret Intelligence Service had a wild idea – send recruits to America, let the CIA train them. It's the special relationship at work. If there are any defections to Moscow then it is the fault of the Yanks. So I spent four years at Langley and another place in Virginia until I could stomach no more. My life was no longer my own. Commitment was one thing but they thought they owned my body. If we tell you – I was instructed – to get in the sack with Comrade X then you do it and smile when he humps you. You flatter him. Say it is the best you ever had. I had a couple of postings until I rebelled. I couldn't stomach it any more. I wasn't going to be Langley's whore. I got out. It left me with bad memories and sometimes a hint of an accent

Fonza stared and without looking away from my face he snapped his fingers. Pietri was at his elbow. Still without looking away, he gestured at the ashtray. "Take it away and empty it. Close the door behind you."

When we were alone, Fonza said: "How can I believe you don't represent somebody? There is no way you can prove it, which is a problem. Now in my work I deal with problems: that is what being one of the two most powerful men in Paris means. In your case it is a question of impressing on you the importance of being straight with me."

"I understand."

"Understanding is not enough," he said, "because you understand with your head. I want you to understand with your stomach."

The move would have been with his knee, under cover of the desk, pressing a button on one of the side panels. No alarm rang: it would have been a pocket electronic call-signal. Three of them arrived in the room virtually simultaneously. Pietri came through the door in a roll across the carpet, ending up with the automatic held two-handed and aimed at me. The knife-artist appeared at a second door, the knife shaft-held above his right shoulder. There were french windows out on to a balcony and the glass smashed as the third man stuck his machine pistol through. I can't judge how long it took them because I don't know when Fonza pressed the button. But it had been less than five seconds since his last sentence about wanting me to understand with my stomach.

Nobody shot. They were waiting for him.

"If you want to walk to the window, *lady*, I'll instruct Carlu not to shoot. You'll see my driver Paoli with a rifle. The gates are shut automatically and my two friends in the car outside are alerted for anybody who climbs over the top. Do you hear the dogs? They are two Alsatians, ones the police were forced to get rid of."

In the wild, movement equals aggression and I felt very strongly the atmosphere of the wild pack. I sat still.

"Alors, filez." Fonza waved a stubby hand in the air and the three men withdrew. His other hand reached out to the Bastos pack. "What is the name of this place you were in last night?"

"The *Prohibition*, off the rue de Buci."

"I don't go slumming."

"They tell me slum landlords drive in Rolls Royces."

He paused, with the flame of his lighter near the tip of his cigarette. "Gently," he said. "The name of your friend."

I told him.

"I have heard of him." He pressed the switch and spoke into the squawkbox. "Gilles Desnos. I think he's blue."

The woman who brought in the file had black hair drawn into a wispy bun at the back of her head and a frowning eagle face. She showed no interest in me: I was something on a piece of furniture.

"And food," he told her.

My friend Desnos had rated a blue dossier, but only a single sheet. I wanted to read it. I was a voyeur, no better than

Crevecoeur. My friend was dead and I wanted to paw through the ashes of his life. Fonza scanned the paper and closed the file.

Bread and *rillettes* were brought and a bottle of wine. "Comte Peraldi," he said, as though the Count were a friend of his. He drank one glass.

"Your friend Desnos seems to have got his life twisted up."

That was all.

We sat in silence while Fonza smoked a cigarette half down and crushed it. One of the external phones rang and he said hallo into it and listened, interrupting once with something I couldn't follow. At the end he said "*D'accord*" into the mouthpiece but looking at me. He replaced the receiver. I wondered who had passed me as clean.

"I think you need a little history lesson," he said. His voice was hoarse, as if fog drifted through his vocal chords. Perhaps he'd had a knife in the throat once but no scar was visible. "1976 was a difficult year for a lot of people in our city. It could have been something to do with Ponia, I can't be certain." Poniatowski had been Minister of the Interior at that time, titular head of police and also confidant to President Giscard. "He ordered the deportation of some North Africans who were peddling stuff around Saint-Séverin and it created something of a vacuum. The concession wasn't much, less than a hundred thousand, but 1976 hadn't been a good year to be in business.

"You know, Paris is just like the world, only on a small scale. And maybe a little distorted, like in those mirrors that make people laugh at fairgrounds. The *quartiers* are a lot of small countries with their own governments who keep order and exact taxes and have little armies. The press, of course, would call it all something else. Then mirroring the real world with the superpowers America and Russia having the dominant say, we have the two families. At that time, 1976, Thierry was the *patron* of the Marsiales, with the three Pavani brothers as his generals. My family, of course, is from Corsica and the *capo* then was

Mufraggi. Try to imagine the Iron Curtain stretching from the porte d'Orléans, down boul Mich, across the river and running up Sébastopol, something like that, not so clear-cut.

"The Saint-Séverin area fell inside Marsiale territory, but only just. So when these Arab hustlers had been sent home Mufraggi decided to probe, move in a few men, organize the bars and street traders one at a time. Like the Cold War, yes? Russia having its adventure in Africa, America showing its muscle in Asia. That's how it began, the shooting war."

He lit another Bastos. It could be too many cigarettes that made his voice rough. I waited, tried not to think, repeating this was just a history lesson, that Paris gang wars had nothing to do with my friend.

"I said it might have been Ponia's doing, a deliberate plan. Certainly the police and the Sûreté were content to let the war go on, providing the casualties were about equal. We lost our *capo* Mufraggi in a bomb explosion under his car. *Plastique* on the exhaust pipe. I don't know how it can have got there because we were extra careful in those days: checking the engine and chassis, decoy cars, changing routes, different headquarters. We lost the entire next rank—Campinchi, Gabriel, Pissard—in a shoot-out at the Café Flore. That was when two of the three Pavani brothers were killed; they'd had a tip-off we were there so surprise was on their side. Even so we got two of them, and the third ten days later in bed with ... Never mind. I'll tell you why I'm positive authority was keeping an eye on events all the time and just letting it burn itself out: because there were two customers wounded in the Café Flore affair and one turned out to be from the Sûreté."

Yes, and hadn't Crevecoeur once showed me a scar he'd collected at the Café Flore? Was it the bullet that had parted his hair? I didn't remember.

"The Marsiales don't all come from Marseille. There were a number of *pieds noirs* returned from Algeria, looking to establish themselves in metropolitan France. You know, we hate the *pieds noirs* more than anybody because the French government gives them resettlement grants and land to farm in Corsica; but they won't give any money to our people for new machinery and irrigation.

"All right, you understand, it was war and a lot of good men on our side had been killed in six weeks. We lost seventeen all told. But on their side it was twenty-eight. And the newspapers were screaming about the Battle of Paris, and saying that Al Capone was alive and well and living in rue Royale. Do you know why the authorities weren't stepping in? Because forty or fifty people somebody high up didn't approve of were dead, and in particular the Marseille connection to Paris was severed. They thought they could stop drugs coming in that way.

"And then it stopped. Shall I tell you the reason? Because the authorities became afraid the Marsiales would be annihilated and it would leave us with the whole of Paris spread out at our feet. They much preferred to have two opposing forces than one dominant one.

"I succeeded Mufraggi as *capo*. On the other side Dugommier had risen to be *patron*. Very early one morning I had a phone call that I was to come, unarmed, with one other man to a truce conference with Dugommier and his lieutenant. The meeting was at Château-Franqui, a village about sixty kilometres north of here. There's nothing there; it's a bloody place, a *bled*. There is a château, nothing grand, outside the village. I was to drive in the east gate at precisely 11 a.m., Dugommier was to come in at the west gate, and we would meet at the front door. No tricks, no possibility of ambush in full daylight, guaranteed neutral territory like Switzerland."

Fonza poured himself another half glass of wine and drank it without hurry.

"It is the Sûreté that owns Château-Franqui, of course. The man who telephoned and made the arrangements and was present at the château to supervise the ceasefire was your friend Desnos."

CHAPTER FIVE

"Have there been any visitors, Mme Boyer?"

"A man called an hour ago, Mlle Cody, and left this."

This was an envelope of coarse paper with the faintest of blue dyes to mask its drab texture. Two or three of the ministries have taken to using recycled paper for unimportant external correspondence. Mme Boyer held the envelope by a corner.

"What was he like?"

"He was not one of your usual men."

There was a smell that lingered in the air round her, of talc and lavender water. She owned three black dresses, with different sleeve lengths to match the seasons. She believed dry cleaning was an extravagance and the fabric of her clothes was permeated with the scent of powder and lavender.

Mme Boyer liked to watch me read letters. "Is it bad news? Nothing too serious?" she would ask, her head tipped back, nostrils testing the air.

I took the letter up to my apartment and it was from a person called Sergeant Bloch. He presented his compliments and said he had given me two telephone calls without success and was now going to deliver this message in case he missed me, time being of the essence. Chief Inspector Crevecoeur had been in touch from Amsterdam and requested a meeting with me that evening. The meeting could not be held in Paris and in order not to disarrange my life, a car and driver would collect me at 19.30 hrs.

I went and lay down on my bed. Reaction to the death of Desnos had set in after Crevecoeur had left me the previous night and I'd slept badly. Now I suffered a second reaction.

If something is too unpalatable, we say it's not true. I found it hard to believe what I'd been told about Desnos. It was intolerable that he might have been sent to spy on me, to scrape a little dirt off the floor of my life, to watch and listen and file his report.

"At 22.30 returned with Subject to her apartment where I stayed until 07.55 next morning. We spent the first hour talking in the living room and I unforcedly raised the subject of the expense of living in the centre of the city. Subject agreed. When I made a joke that, having lived in the United States, perhaps she was supported by alimony, Subject did not laugh but replied she did not approve of lawyers and the American divorce industry. Subject is not entirely devoid of a sense of humour, however. She said there was an old American saying that one lawyer in town starved, but two lawyers in town became rich.

"Again I turned the conversation to Subject's means of financial support and remarked she obviously wasn't getting her money through being a lawyer. She agreed and was silent and then volunteered that she had a legacy from an uncle (compare Subject's 77/A9101). Subject then finished her drink and suggested we go to bed. I had been ready to press her on this point, according to instructions, but Subject was quite straightforward in her attitude.

"Subject undressed in front of me in the bedroom, where there is a double bed, and left the light on. We had intercourse twice. In the throes of passion, Subject uttered some words of an erotic nature, common to such situations, but nothing of wider significance. At approximately 01.45 Subject switched out the light. Before sleeping, I engaged Subject in conversation for about thirty minutes, complimenting her on her skill at lovemaking and trying to elicit the names of male friends from her. Subject warned me not to snoop like a private detective and I judged it better to leave the matter alone.

"During the night I was able, under guise of visiting the bathroom, to search Subject's desk in the living room. There was nothing that gave any indication of current illegal activities, nor of any connection with the Central Intelligence Agency, any East European espionage organization, nor any French department. There was a personal communication on US State Department paper from the man Martin, but this is the letter dated 5 August (no year added) which you already have a copy of.

"I was unable to discover the pistol that has been mentioned.

"I woke Subject at 07.00 and we had intercourse again. According to the tactical plan I asked her if she would like to go away in the New Year to ski and she agreed. I offered to supply Subject with a ticket and she refused, saying she would pay for herself. The Department's budget will not, therefore, have to meet her direct expenses and I hope will see its way to allowing me extra latitude."

It would be typed out, in triplicate, on the faint bluish paper. Crevecoeur's file on me would be a little fatter.

The curtain kept the room in semi-darkness. I tried to be rational about it because love, hate and anger all corrode our thinking. But the emotional impact was overwhelming: Fonza said Gilles Desnos had been employed by the Sûreté Nationale. In which case he had been, to use the Agency's unofficial term, a "bed and board". He had employed a sexual relationship to gain information. Crevecoeur had set him to spy on me and the idea was distasteful.

With Crevecoeur anything was possible.

CHAPTER SIX

CHATEAU-FRANQUI
WEDNESDAY 21 MARCH
8.40 P.M.

We drove through Noailles and turned left off the *route nationale*, passed a Total service station and a concrete warehouse, fences on to stark ploughed fields, an abandoned dung-spreader. Perhaps it was five minutes further that we turned again, right at a sign that read Château-Franqui. The village was three houses. The château was over a rise in the land, a fallow wilderness that would grow sugarbeet.

It was dark when we arrived. Crevecoeur would have arranged for me to arrive in the dark.

The chauffeur showed a pass at the gates, somebody put a flashlight in our faces, and then we were admitted. The drive bent through a thick patch of trees, still winter-naked in the headlamps, and curved round to stop in front of the château. It was without distinction, a country house put up by some industrial baron in the last century.

The Sûreté would have more than one establishment near Paris to talk to people away from snoopers and lawyers. Château-Franqui was the place where Desnos had arranged the truce between the warring gangs and perhaps that was why Crevecoeur had chosen it to meet me.

Sergeant Bloch got out from beside the driver to lead the way to a side door with a minuscule entrance porch. I paused long enough to get the feel of the place. The bare branches of the trees stood out against the night sky, black on black. No lights showed at the windows, shutters closed and blinds drawn inside as if it were a wartime blackout.

"This way, Mlle Cody."

There was no hint of anything living anywhere. No voice, no dog, no other car. Only, I had the feeling I was being observed.

"Mlle Cody..."

A man in uniform was waiting when I reached the side door. He checked my face against a photograph on a clipboard, asking me to step forward into the shaft of light from the corridor behind him. When I passed I saw he hadn't consulted the head-and-shoulders shot from my residence application that would be on file at the Sûreté. The photo appeared to have been taken at a café: I could see the sticker on the plate-glass window behind me advertising Rhum Negrita. I was shocked: not just because it was more evidence of what pains Crevecoeur had gone to in order to find out more about me, but because I hadn't noticed. Tourists with cameras are everywhere in Paris but after they've finished with you at Virginia Training you are supposed always to notice when you are being followed. How could I have grown so lax?

"Have you...?" the man in uniform began.

"She's okay," Sergeant Bloch told him.

I was a parcel, special delivery, nothing more.

Crevecoeur was in a high-ceilinged reception room, with the curtains tight closed, diffused light from standard lamps with heavy shades, bulky overstuffed chairs, a couple of paintings of mountainscapes. Incongruously, an English dartboard hung on a pockmarked area of wall. He'd been talking to a man in army uniform as I came into the room and he rose to greet me, make the introduction, until he saw the look in my eyes.

"Leave us, Georges," he said.

The officer already had his right hand half extended for the French ritual and he faltered, looking from Crevecoeur to me to his useless hand. He shrugged.

"Later," the officer said. "Time is evaporating, remember." He left.

Perhaps I should have thought about his remark then. The point is, I didn't. I felt bitterness because of Desnos's deception and if he'd been alive my anger would have been directed at him. Emotion was corroding my ability to think.

An hour I'd had in the back of the car, first in the curdled traffic in the city centre, then the Nürburgring of the peripheral road with commuters flashing neurotic messages with their lights, the cars thinning as we headed north; and I'd sat in the back seat, feeding my anger that Crevecoeur should try to involve me in his kidnapping while for months he'd had me under surveillance, had insinuated someone into my life.

"That was Colonel Georges Messeix. Heard of him?"

I didn't answer and he didn't elaborate.

"Thank you for coming here. I hope it was not too inconvenient."

His head tipped to one side, trying to read my face.

"I have to go to Germany tomorrow, very early, and this is convenient for the airfield at Beauvais."

He turned and pressed a bell by the unlit fireplace.

"I suppose it works. It would have in the old days. The gentleman who built it had a factory in Amiens, making confectionery, and this was his country residence."

Crevecoeur didn't like the silence and cleared his throat.

A steward in a white jacket came in with a tray. There was ham that had started its life in a can, foil-wrapped quarters of Camembert, bread and miniature packs of butter. He set the tray on a table, muttered something and left.

"What did he say? *Bon appétit?*" Crevecoeur tried a smile. There was a strand of black tobacco lodged between his front teeth. He flicked a finger at the food. "Disgusting. You'd think we lived in an uncivilized country. At least we have whisky." He took the bottle from a shelf. "What have you found out?"

He poured the whisky, added ice cubes and moved in front of me.

I said: "Desnos is dead."

He nodded. "I meant, what have you found out about the kidnapping of Simone Poelsma?"

"Gilles Desnos, who was supposed to be my friend, is dead. Last night I saw him murdered. And today I find out he wasn't my friend, he was employed by you."

He grunted. "Desnos worked for the SN. That doesn't stop him having a private life. A cop is allowed to have girl friends. We're not monks."

"You planted him. He was your spy. You wanted something on me and he was the one who was going to nose out some smelly little secret and when you ... "

His anger stopped me dead in my tracks. There were black smudges of tiredness under his eyes, a grey pallor to his skin, twin spots of red on his cheeks that could have come from the whisky. He'd drained the glass while I spoke and now the words spewed out of him.

"Shut up, Cody. You make me sick when you come on like a Sunday-school teacher. You're concerned with the purity of your soul and nothing else exists in the world. I asked your help in finding a little girl because it was something you could do and I couldn't, and you've done nothing. These people could cut off Simone's hair and then her ears and her toes and pull out the fingernails and slice off her nose, but all you're worried about is whether Desnos made a report about how you bounced on the mattress. I knew about you and him because I saw pictures of you together on holiday and I warned him, don't get in too deep because Cody's a cold one and runs a life that is rather foolish and even dangerous. If you think that's how I programme a check on suspects, you're goddam stupider than I thought. Think about it. Think about the last couple of months. Wasn't Desnos holding back from you? I wasn't pushing him to find the dirt under your carpet because he was too valuable to me in other ways. Well? Did he try to burrow in close?"

He stared and stared, and reached for the bottle again.

"Are you going to answer?" Crevecoeur spoke almost perfect English, learned from his spell at the Washington embassy, but in his anger his accent slipped. "Well?"

"If he held back it was because he found nothing to incriminate me."

"Oh sweet Jesus. You're so incriminated already I could have you driven to Orly and put on the first jet out of here. You trained with the CIA and I now have full details in your file in rue des Saussaies. You say you got out, and maybe I believe you and maybe I don't, but you trying convincing a judge. You did a job in Berlin eighteen months ago and it was your CIA buddy Frank Duraine who drove you to Tegel airport to fly you out. You were employed directly by the CIA in Istanbul. You have an account with the Kredietbank in Luxembourg with nearly fifty thousand dollars in it. Perhaps you've closed the account now and moved it to Lichtenstein or the Cayman Islands. Give me a couple of days and I'll trace it and then the tax people will make a meal of you. So don't talk to me about your innocent little life."

Crevecoeur had the gift of selecting half-truths and twisting them until the ugly side was exposed. No successful security cop is without it.

He poured more whisky, the bottle rattling against the glass. The sound of his shaking hand seemed to anger him all over again and he jerked back to me.

"You know nothing of me or my work or the complexities of what we do. Among the other things your lover Desnos was engaged on was trying to find out something about Poelsma. He

44

had to leave all the final arrangements for the opening night of that club to his partner because from the moment the girl was snatched he was concentrating on Poelsma. Shall I tell you why? Because Poelsma also worked for me."

There was a chair behind me and I shuffled until I felt the fat cushion against the back of my knees. I sat slowly and sipped my drink.

There are ten or more organizations in France with overlapping responsibilities for security and intelligence and so forth. They are all engaged in surveilling embassies and snooping on informants and political activists and *Le Canard Enchaîné* and each other. The Deuxième Bureau peeps over the shoulder of SDECE. The Sûreté taps the phones of DST. Now it seemed the Sûreté spied on itself.

Crevecoeur looked at the food again and got out his Gitanes. He inhaled deeply, trying to smother his anger. "Goddam, why do you have to have everything spelled out?"

I said: "If you need to ask that question, then I can't give you an answer you'd understand."

"What the hell is that supposed to mean?"

He made a tour of the room, touching things vaguely, and sat down and said: "Poelsma was in my pocket, a useful man, resourceful, hard, shrewd. His association with the Sûreté Nationale began about six years ago. His cover was excellent because it was true. He was a rich entrepreneur and travelled a lot in connection with his diamond broker business: America, England, Hong Kong and more recently the Middle East."

"What did he do for you?"

He thought about it some time. "You must appreciate my position," he said. "I sympathize with you: you don't want to leap in the dark. But you know, I must be allowed my little secrets." He tried a smile again. With others you notice the upward turn of the lips, the softening of the eyes, the creases in the cheeks. When Crevecoeur smiled you noticed the teeth. "I'll put it in general terms: in his business Poelsma was able to move quite large sums of money round the world. It was natural and no bank or treasury would suspect anything wrong. We are an organization that is officially only concerned with matters in France, but boundaries mean so little now. If I have an interest in Monsieur Duclos in Paris and then he makes a plane tour to Belgrade and Aden and Tripoli, I'm interested in his journey too. We are like the FBI—have you any notion how many 'legal advisers' there are at the American embassy in Paris? No matter. The point is we have regular payments for salaries, rents, so on, and regular channels of payments. But we can also have a sudden and secret need to make extraordinary payments to persons in Chicago or Cambodia or wherever. You can see the convenience of a man like Poelsma who could legitimately move a hundred thousand dollars, or walk straight through customs with a case of diamonds chained to his wrist."

"Obviously he was a reliable man?"

"Worse than that, he was trusted. His security classification put him fairly high up the scale." Crevecoeur raised a hand to shoulder height and it no longer trembled. "You won't know how we organize security-checking. It is different from the CIA and we don't have the ruthless ways with traitors that the Russians do, but we are clever in our own fashion. A little bit of jargon: someone permanent like me is referred to as a *pensionnaire,* a 'boarder', and I won't go into that because it's not relevant. Someone like Poelsma, who is not within the career structure, is called a *contractant,* a 'contractor'. For them there is the system of positive and negative clearance. Negative is the usual series of traces run through files and personal inquiries, banks, employers, school, university, military service records, union or political affiliation, foreign travel, neighbours, friends. Routine. When we know the story of his life, the recruit is submitted to positive clearance. He is sent by the Intendant (Contractants) on three missions of increasing temptation. He believes he is already accepted but in fact he is being monitored for incompetence or contacts with an opposition network. We begin with a mission to a safe country, say Norway or Costa Rica. I'll come on to the nature of the mission in a moment. The second is to a communist country, say Vietnam, making contact with a low-level operative. The third is somewhat sensitive and fluid, say Mauretania or Lebanon, and there an agent provocateur tries to recruit him for the other side. Only those who resist the pressure *and report it* on their return to France are given positive clearance.

"Now Poelsma achieved positive security clearance while I was at the Washington embassy. I knew nothing of him until I returned to Paris, since when he's been working for me, very useful. I never thought to check his clearance until Sunday after his girl had been kidnapped and I came across a remarkable thing in his personnel file. His first positive security mission had been to Washington while I was actually working there. It was during the Watergate period and there was some fairy tale about his making payment to a member of Nixon's staff for a transcript of the tapes. I find it a curious detail that I never met him, that I was not warned he was coming to Washington, nor asked for facilities to monitor him."

Crevecoeur poured himself more Scotch. It was Cutty Sark, one of those light whiskies that tiptoes up and suddenly slugs the back of your head. He sighed and screwed back the cap.

"When you see someone in Security drink too much, there's somebody who's blown their nerve. Listen, I was in Holland today and the President's advance party flew in. That's the American President, not mine. There were one hundred and sixty of them. They started in right there at Amsterdam airport, walking round with two-way radios, measuring angles of fire from rooftops, running metal detectors over the tarmac, moving me out of the office I'd been allocated because they needed it for emergency telecommunications. If regular communications are cut, I want you to know there is a US Marines sergeant who can sprint to the emergency equipment from anywhere on the President's route at the airport and World War Three would only be delayed by a maximum of one minute forty seconds.

"Tomorrow morning I fly to Bonn to liaise with the German Chancellor's security people because our President will be having a heart-to-heart with him before the conference.

"And while these great affairs of international politics drag on, I am worrying about a nine-year-old girl who's missing."

He stood before me like a schoolteacher in front of a class.

"Item: the kidnappers call Poelsma by his first name, as if they knew him.

"Item: they deliver a note to Poelsma, which Poelsma does not tell me about.

"Item: nanny repeats the note to me and it demands co-operation not money.

"Item: Poelsma's security file has a prima facie error in it; and the man who gave him clearance cannot be questioned because he was the victim of a car crash, very conveniently, in the August of that year; and maybe the file has been falsified.

"Item: your friend Desnos who was interesting himself in Poelsma was murdered; and only someone inside the Sûreté Nationale would know what he was doing."

I suddenly felt very tired. "What do you expect me to do, for God's sake? It's not my job."

"What can I do?" he replied. "And it *is* my job. My nose tells me Poelsma is being blackmailed. I have lost one man, and so have you, because he started enquiries. So who do I trust in my organization?"

"You want someone to clean out French Security?"

"That would be impossible. Why do you think France has so many security outfits? Why do you imagine new ones keep springing up? The Africa Bureau, Salut Spécial, the Bureau for the Development of Agriculture, all the ones with obscure names. They start up and they're clean, and within six months they're riddled like all the others. But if you get the girl back then there's no pressure on Poelsma, and without pressure there can be no blackmail."

"Where is Poelsma?"

He shrugged. "Evaporated. He used our Transport Facility to make a reservation on an Air Inter flight to Nice on Tuesday morning and Desnos went to the airport to monitor his departure. He never checked in."

Crevecoeur was wandering again, touching things, feeling reality. He looked tired. Half an hour before he'd looked angry. Then again last night he'd come across smooth with his hints about Duraine. Also he'd been filled with concern for a missing child. And before that he'd looked full of confidence. There was no single Crevecoeur. He didn't exist.

"Okay," I told him.

For a moment I thought he was going to kiss me.

Crevecoeur was called to the phone. It's an old trick: someone would be at a spyhole observing my actions and facial expressions.

I sat where I could watch the door and used the time on my own.

There were contradictions and I turned them over in my mind because it is from contradictions you learn so much. The most obvious one was the easiest disposed of. If Crevecoeur had so distrusted me, if he'd had me followed and photographed and had slipped an agent into my life, why was he now trying to get me to do a job? The point was that for months he had tried to get a lever against me because he desperately wanted his gun back; now he had switched, decided to make use of me. Security organizations never admit using freelances but it is common in certain situations, because a freelance is expendable and can always be denied. In this instance it was different: I wasn't contaminated like his department.

I pushed the idea round and it seemed plausible. Though with Crevecoeur you could never be certain.

The other contradiction was in myself and it wasn't so easy to resolve. I'd maintained I would never do a job for him and in an instant, without thinking, almost on impulse, I had changed. It was an emotional response and I had to face that. Nothing to do with his heavy hints about dropping the tax inspectorate on me or revoking my residence permit. Nothing to do with helping his internal security problems. I tried to persuade myself it was to help a terrified little girl.

Crevecoeur came back through the door. His face looked eerie as if he'd gone nights without sleep. He went like an automaton to the Cutty Sark bottle and then spun the metal cap closed and poured some Perrier water instead.

He said: "The Minister of the Interior." He drank the Perrier and put the tumbler down. "He's on his way to see me, which is amazing. I told him I was engaged in interrogation and couldn't leave Château-Franqui." Crevecoeur gave his smile like the end of January. "The President is worried—no, the President is never worried—is concerned about security arrangements for the conference. He's heard some chat about possible riots." He shrugged. "So some students are going to let off steam. Oh, and there's been a leak about the agenda: the Israeli Premier has vetoed negotiations about Jerusalem. Another thing: one of the Egyptian delegation is an observer for the Palestinians and if the Israelis don't object to him, some marxist splinter group will. But you're not interested in politics, are you? I envy you."

No, I was concerned with the death of Desnos. It was that which I was reluctant to face, my reason for agreeing to help.

There must be another word than vengeance. Justice sounds less ugly.

Our trudging footsteps echoed down the carpetless corridor.

"Here's a little thing that might interest you."

He opened the door and we passed into a sombre panelled room. There were a long, mahogany dining table and ten chairs.

"Look," he said, pointing to a little brass plaque screwed into the high-backed chair at the head of the table.

I bent forward and up again. "I don't speak German."

"No, no, just the name."

I leaned down again to read the name in Gothic script in the centre of the plaque.

"He was here?"

"Yes," Crevecoeur said, gratified at my surprise. "he made the journey from Berlin to establish a forward command post for the hop over the Channel to Britain. For the best part of a week Château-Franqui was his headquarters while Goering was dictating the battle against the Spitfires from his railway carriage outside Calais. It was in the fall of 1940. He could have stayed in Paris, but he considered it a sewer. And then, while he was waiting here for Goering to master the air, the RAF penetrated as far as Berlin and dropped a few bombs. While he was absent, you understand, that was what infuriated him. So he returned to Berlin, ordered Goering to stop attacking English airfields and aircraft factories, and bomb London as a punishment. A fatal error of judgement: this was the closest he ever got to England."

"The house didn't belong to the Sûreté Nationale then?"

"Oh no. The Gestapo had it. When they left in 1944 we simply took over from them."

CHAPTER SEVEN

In chess a player edges a pawn forward one square or two. That is how the game starts. There is no other way.

Thereafter there are a myriad possibilities. The pawn may be taken, or be forgotten, or place the opponent's king in check, or be sacrificed.

I was Crevecoeur's pawn.

It was late when I was dropped. I watched the lights of the car move away from the kerb and caught the flash of white as Sergeant Bloch's face passed under the street light. A drizzle had started, clammy and depressing, and the night was closing down. There would be life on the boulevards until two or three but few were out in rue Saint-André-des-Arts for pleasure. Neon slipped restlessly over the wet paving, blue and green and red.

Light shone through the fugged up window of the Café Charlot. It never closed and you could tell the time of night from its clientele. At six in the evening there were pastis-drinkers snorting a couple after work. At nine there were those who realized it was too late to return home for dinner. At midnight it was the drunks and homeless. By two in the morning they had been pushed out and it was the occasional thin-cheeked student, a bleary party from a club calling in for a last glass, a girl on a stool smoking a filtertip cigarette and watching the door in the mirror.

Between four and five was the only dead time, and then the first-comers in blue arrived, blowing out their cheeks and saying *bon jour* a little too loudly. Raoul took over behind the bar and shook hands with truck drivers, porters from the little market round the corner, butchers, remembering who drank *café-rhum* and who wanted a *coup de rouge*. That was the beginning of the day.

He was watching me.

It was gone midnight. I was tired, cold; the anger I'd felt earlier had drained away leaving me dispirited. The body and emotions were approaching the low point of their cycle and this was accentuated because I had eaten nothing since Fonza's bread and *rillettes* in the middle of the day. There was food in my apartment—eggs, cheese, salami—but I wanted to put off the moment I went there because of the ghosts.

He had a patch of window cleared of steam.

I was willing to put up with the drunks and the suggestions of the strays who were hoping for a home for the night because at least the people in the Café Charlot were alive. The bread in the sandwiches would be stale, like the air, but there would be no silence to haunt.

The silence would come later, in the dark, and there would be no way to fill it. It would be there tonight and tomorrow night and until the scars filled over.

The opaque condensation framed the eyes and it was when I was no more than a couple of paces from the café door that I recognized who it was. The clear area was the size of a postcard and the message in the eyes was cold.

He was the one who'd been so sharp with the knife at Fonza's house, the one whose pink tongue led an independent existence. I didn't know his name.

He could have come to collect a little tribute owing to Fonza, for the Café Charlot was in Fonza's sector; but I was too old to believe in bedtime stories.

The knife-artist was there because of me.

I kept my pace steady and passed the entrance. I didn't think there'd been a flash-flood of recognition on my face but he'd know it had gone wrong within three seconds when I didn't bang open the door. As a precaution he would already have paid for his drink and by now he'd be pushing back his chair. I started to run.

My apartment was out of bounds because there could be a couple more of them waiting behind the curtains or in the dark at the turn of the stairs. There was one of those lulls you begin to get in city traffic after midnight and in the hole in the noise I heard my shoes on the pavement and then the café door open behind me. There was a little burst of warm voices and laughter, and the sound cut dead as the door slammed shut.

I was only thirty metres or so in front of him and there was no possibility of reaching the crossroad ahead or of sprinting to the other side of rue Saint-André-des-Arts. If he was present on knife-business, thirty metres was the top limit of an effective throw, even for an expert; but he would have a gun with a silencer and no one would hear my body roll over and lie still. He wouldn't even need the silencer. How often had I heard a car backfire in the night and thought nothing.

I grabbed at the corner of the building and swung left. It was just an unlit alley running between tall buildings. No name. No exit.

Abruptly I stopped and listened and there were no footsteps.

I'd been down the alley before because it was insurance to explore the local geography and I knew there was no low wall at the end or friendly overhanging branch into a garden. But even a dead-end alley has to have something.

I palmed two doorhandles and that was no luck.

Again I listened and there were no footsteps.

Error on my part? False recognition?

No. He was a professional in his field and he'd have checked the alley and known it had no exit. He was taking time, walking with care.

A final door led into the building at the end of the alley. Locked. There was a last window. It had bars. No lights shone. The buildings stored timber and sacks of charcoal and kitchenware and were only occupied during the working day.

A tapping had begun on my right. A downpipe came from the guttering on the roof and the drizzle had started the first drops down it. I estimated twenty metres up the drainpipe to the roof. The screws securing the structure to the bricks had long rusted and that was no hope either.

There was the noise of a car engine and lights flashed at the end of the alley and were gone.

I saw the twin eyes glint green in the brief light.

There were two trashcans set on either side of the door at the end of the alley. The cat had taken a fish-head out of one and had frozen, tensed, watching me.

I'd been nine or ten seconds in the alley and perhaps I had five seconds more before the knife-artist appeared at the entrance. I had nothing else but the cat.

"*Eh b'en, minou, que t'es joli, toi, alors minou viens ici, n'as pas peur.*" It wasn't the words that mattered. It was the tone of voice, soft, soothing.

At the end the cat took fright and dashed for freedom but I'd got one hand on its tail and then the other grasped tight round its neck and ears as it spat at me. I could do nothing about the claws.

The trashcans were modern heavy-duty plastic with lids that did a short turn to lock. I dropped the cat in and there was no way it could dislodge the lid and escape.

Time was running out and I had to sink behind the shelter of the other trashcan and trust to curiosity.

The alley was obliterated in darkness but the human eye adapts, the iris expanding to admit maximum data. Given four minutes, the knife-artist would develop night vision and begin to distinguish areas of light among the shadows. My dark sweater and dark slacks were no problem but Caucasian skin is at a disadvantage in a situation like that. I tucked my hands under my armpits. The worst was I couldn't look: I had to lower my face and wait.

He knew I was there. He knew I was alert to him. He was very wary.

His shoes had rubber soles and he came on the balls of his feet, infinitely slowly. He was very good. The first I heard of him was no more than a couple of steps away, his foot scrunching on a metal bottle-cap and stopping in the instant. The silence took over again.

He was assessing.

Before fighting an enemy, a cat will screech in an attempt to psych its opponent into submission. When caught up a tree, a cat will wail for human aid. When cornered by an animal larger than itself, a cat will hiss and spit. But when trying to escape from a trap a cat utters no sound because it serves no useful purpose.

The cat's paws were scrabbling but the heavy-duty plastic bin and the rubbish inside muffled the sound. It was no more than a body moving restlessly in a confined space.

And still the knife-artist hesitated. I couldn't look at him but he'd be checking the barred window and the padlocked door and then having to give credence to the evidence of his ears. He was searching for a human, there was no means of escape, and sounds of a body came from the cramped confines of the trash-can. Conclusion: the human was hiding under the lid.

The tiniest sound came from the metal bottle-top and I knew he'd lifted his foot and was moving. I raised my face and he was two-thirds turned away from me, reaching for the lid with his left hand, his right hand gripping the knife, shaft in the palm, blade between thumb and forefinger. It is the grip an alleyfighter uses when intending to slip in under the ribcage. I rose in the same movement because I knew he'd notice the changing light pattern in peripheral vision and I would only have one opportunity to get the knife away from him before he turned.

I didn't want to end up on the dead-end side of him so I made the jump-kick with my left foot. He was actually starting to turn into me as the instep of my shoe connected with his elbow and the impact was increased. I heard the knife hit the wall and rebound on to the ground and skitter away into the darkness. The sound of pain and surprise came from deep in his throat.

I was placed on the freedom side of him now and it was my best chance to make a break while he was confused and worried about the loss of his power-source. No knife-fighter is at ease with the knife out of reach.

But he was more than a knife-fighter and he'd trained in more than the back streets of Bastia. He'd grunted at the shooting pain in the elbow but he didn't move to rub the bruised bone. He swept his arm in an arc that caught my shoulder as I began to run. The stone blocks in the alley were rain-greasy and my shoes lost their purchase and I ended in a skid against the brick wall. I landed on hands and knees and in the split second before I got up he started his move to cut off my line of escape.

He was stocky, dark, a little Napoleon like all Corsicans. None the less, he was stronger than I. He had lost his knife but I had lost the element of surprise. If I were to have a chance against him it was only by making a crass move and reversing his expectations.

As he darted to cut off my escape I went the other way towards the dead-end of the alley. The move was against reason and by the time he'd checked himself he'd moved into the sideways position where he was vulnerable to a *kosotogari*. I reached in to grasp his upper arms and stepped closer, turning on the ball of my right foot and bearing down and back on him with my hands. It is the easiest of the ankle throws once your opponent is in the sideways position, and there was little he could do. I could feel his balance breaking as I curved my body and brought my left foot in a swift jab against the back of his ankle, and the throw was complete, his body revolving as if there were an axle through his hips. If it had been in contest conditions I would have followed down to pin him on the mat but there were no judges awarding points and I dropped him.

I should have learned from his first move. He was fast in his reflexes where others would have needed brain-time.

He caught at me as I turned to run, one hand punching my heel, and I went sprawling. I scrambled up very fast because I feared him getting to close quarters and applying any sort of strength hold. He was already reaching for the trashcan and it came at me as I started forward again. The can caught me at the back of the knees and I went over again, the lid bursting open and filth flying round.

And now he closed. He came from behind as I was on the ground, his body flopping over my head, elbows dug into my ribs, gripping at my belt. I twisted left and that was no good and then right. He had got his feet out of line and I was able to roll him on his back, his skull knocking against the stone.

I broke loose. I got my feet on the ground and jack-knifed upright and he followed a split second behind. There was broken glass and orange peel and soggy newspaper underfoot as I aimed for the pale light at the entrance to the alley, and the raucous yell of the cat distracted me. The man grasped my right hand round the wrist and stretched as he went to ground, pulling me with him, one leg over my neck, my elbow braced over his other knee. I could move if I wanted to break my elbow joint. I was still.

We lay on the ground and I could feel the sweat on my wrist from his hands, but not enough to slip free. There was the sound of our breathing.

The seconds drew out and nobody came. Why should they? Bloody cat at the trashcans again.

He said: "Why did you attack?"

I said: "You had the knife out."

"You were leading me into the alley. It was a trap."

"Why were you waiting for me? Why did you follow?"

"The *capo's* orders."

We caught our breath. I tried easing the pressure on the joint and he responded by raising his knee.

He said: "Don't start again."

"We can't spend the night here."

"Well, understand this. Nobody wins a fight against the *capo*. Don't try to escape because you've nowhere to run to. The *capo* has pals everywhere."

"Why did Fonza send you?"

"He's heard a whisper about Poelsma. He's flown but he's been seen. As I said, the *capo* has pals everywhere."

He let go of me and I squatted on the wet paving stones, rubbing my wrist. There was stickiness there and it was partly the sweat from his hands and partly blood that the cat's claws had drawn.

I made no move to go. It was what he'd said; not what he'd said about not escaping, but about Poelsma.

He scraped round on his hands and knees in the dark and recovered his knife. That made him happier: no matter how skilled he is in other directions, a knife-artist without his blade feels like a castrato.

It was harder for me to recover my self-respect. He was bigger and stronger than me; he'd started armed; the light had been bad, the conditions cramped, the ground rain-slippery. But those were excuses. In training school in Virginia they wrote it in block capitals on the blackboard: *NEVER OUTFIGHT WHEN YOU CAN OUTSMART.* Because someone somewhere sometime will outfight you into the grave. This alley could have been my grave because I hadn't been smart enough.

There was the question crowding everything else out of my mind and I had to ask it: "How do you know about Poelsma?"

A car flashed past the entrance to the alley and in the brief glow I saw his face, a sideways look with nothing in it for me. "Come on," he said, "let's go."

"I want to know."

"Listen," he said. "You asked the *capo* about Desnos but you didn't say you were also interested in a guy called Poelsma. That was careless."

"Who told Fonza?"

"A pal."

It was the third time he'd used the word *copain*. And that is what de Gaulle bequeathed to France: a system run by *copains* and *coquins,* pals and rascals, the politicians, the police, the bosses, the unions, the underworld, all with their hands in each other's pockets, rubbing their palms together.

"The *capo* has instructed me to help you," he went on.

"I work alone." I hate dependence on others, being bound to their actions, tripped by their mistakes.

"I have my instructions. In any case you cannot work alone because you do not know where to look."

"Then tell me." I very much wanted to know where Poelsma had gone: since he gave the appearance of knowing the kidnappers, he'd go to talk to them.

Another car came past and I saw his face with a frown on it. I was querying the *capo*'s divine right and it worried him. His pink tongue came out, searching, searching.

We returned to the darkness.

"Come on," he said. "Someone will see us."

"A couple of lovers," I replied. "Tell me."

"Poelsma has gone to Holland."

"I would have checked there at once. He has a house in Amsterdam."

"He hasn't been near his house." He started cracking the knuckles of one of his hands.

"I'll find him."

"Possibly you'd find him on your own. But the *capo* is concerned about Desnos being shot by the Marsiales and Poelsma skipping to Holland. If the Marsiales are involved, then it's our business."

"You don't have any business in Holland," I said.

"We have pals. We have pals in a lot of cities, but particularly in Amsterdam."

He didn't say more but he didn't have to. Amsterdam had become the central clearing house for drugs from the east.

The whole situation froze my blood. I squatted in a squalid little alley in the Sixth arrondissement in Paris and felt the chill start in my belly and stretch out through my body. In twenty-four hours I had witnessed a friend gunned down, I had been hooked into a kidnapping and a missing courier for French Security, and now I found myself under the hot breath of one of the Paris street-gangs.

My eyes had adjusted to the dark and I saw his tongue roaming in front of his mouth. He started work on the knuckles of his other hand.

"So I'm coming with you," he said.

CHAPTER EIGHT

He slipped a pudgy hand inside my pants and began to feel around. He had piggy eyes, greedy at the sight of black nylon. There was a flabbiness under his chin and a tightness of the shirt across his belly where the beer took him. His eyes lifted and checked reaction on my face.

"Okay," he intoned, and made the hieroglyph with pale blue chalk.

I was doing up my zip and he turned his attention to the man behind.

"*Hebt U iets aan to geven?*"

There was a time when they used to say things like "Have a nice stay", but after four million times the words curdle your tongue.

"Anything to declare?"

The man behind replied "*Rien*", but they made him open his bag anyway. The luggage search was rigorous and the lines stretched back irritably from the hastily set up trestle tables. Against the wall there were police in uniform with shiny white holsters on their hips, and two men in Dacron suits and clipped hair shared back-of-the-hand secrets.

Security had been just as tight at Passport Control. There had been two men, one in dark blue uniform and one in plain clothes. The uniformed one held my passport: and checked my face against the photo. I'd had my hair longer and tied back in a bunch when the photo had been taken and the uniformed one told me to pull the hair back off my forehead.

"Why are you coming to the Netherlands?"

"Tourist."

"How long are you staying?"

"Three or four days."

"Where are you staying?"

"Amsterdam. I'm going to the VVV to check hotel rooms."

"How much money are you bringing in?"

I'd opened my bag and showed him the Amex travel cheques and the five hundred dollars I keep in the spine of *Larousse Gastronomique* in the kitchen of my apartment.

Throughout this petty interrogation, the man in plain clothes flipped through cards in a box file. He nodded and his companion found a blank page in my passport and branded it with his little diamond-shaped stamp.

The man in line behind me also answered tourist. I wondered why they asked such pointless questions.

The man behind me had also been in the row behind me on the Air France 727. And before that in the taxi behind me on the way to Charles de Gaulle airport. And before that in the alley.

He'd told me his name was Sarasini. He'd told me his first name too but I didn't take it in. He'd spent the night in my apartment but we'd never be on first-name terms. Having Sarasini like a dog at my heels made me uneasy. He could have been a bodyguard or a prison warder and maybe there was no difference.

I went through doors to the concourse and followed Sarasini's instructions. There was a KLM desk over to my right and I weaved my way across. The girl in the uniform put on the smile they issued with it.

"*Dag, Juffrouw.*"

"I want to catch a connection to London."

"Our next flight departs at eleven o'clock. But," she glanced at the clock, "British Airways have a flight in forty minutes. You just have time to check in."

"There's no delay with the weather?"

"The weather?" She shook her brown curls, not understanding.

"I heard there was bad weather at London."

"No, we have no delays."

I said thank you.

Sarasini was putting his pink tongue out at a TV monitor with some flight information on it and then he turned and walked away. In one hand he carried an airline overnight bag and in the other a black attaché case. I'd wondered how he would pass the security checks at Charles de Gaulle, with the knife strapped to his forearm. But the attaché case had an extended handle that broke apart, the knife was cushioned inside the metal frame and nothing suspicious had shown on the X-ray screen.

I threaded my way back through the crowd. Again there were police, standing against walls, studying faces. One man in a trench-coat had a walkie-talkie to his lips. Nerves were showing already because of the Middle East conference starting at the week-end.

I passed through to the coffee-shop as a flight to Rome was called and took my cup to a table vacated by a family with two fractious boys. A young Indonesian man wheeled up a trolley and cleared the debris from my table with the slowness all airport staff develop.

I didn't have to wait long.

A middle-aged man holding a cup made his way across from the counter.

"Is this seat free?" His English had the throaty Dutch intonation. He wore a grey suit and struggled with a coat over one arm, a briefcase and a copy of *Nieuwe Rotterdamse Courant* under the other.

"Yes."

He stirred at the coffee while the Indonesian empted the ashtray and moved to the next table.

"Do you know", he asked, "if there is any delay on the flights to London?"

Yes, he'd been the one at the end of the KLM counter. I hadn't been positive because there was nothing memorable in the sandy hair and muddy eyes, and he hadn't been carrying the newspaper then. If he liked to vary the image, then inside the briefcase there'd be a squashy hat and steel-framed glasses with plain lenses.

People were taking a lot more precautions since the murder of Desnos.

"I don't think there's any delay."

"No trouble with the weather?"

"No report of any," I told him. "What time is your flight?"

"Just a minute." He opened the briefcase and it contained a woollen scarf, a copy of *Newsweek* and a collapsible umbrella. He picked out a KLM timetable. "I think it's eleven o'clock. Yes, eleven."

"There's a British Airways flight in thirty-five minutes. If you hurry, you'll have time to transfer."

"That's very good. I shall be early for my business appointment. Thank you, miss, you've been most helpful."

He didn't hurry. Nobody would have paid him any attention as he gathered up his raincoat and briefcase. He left the KLM timetable but he didn't need it any more.

I drank some coffee and when I put the cup down I turned over the timetable. In the blank space left for the travel agent's rubber stamp it was marked: Hotel Excelsior, Huidenstraat 28, Amsterdam.

It got stuck, and it took a second go for the back page of the timetable to flush down the toilet.

Outside, the army had taken over.

In Holland you can tell the conscript boys because they wear their hair long. Professionals are the same in any country, the clipped hair, the flat features, the stare over your shoulder.

As I came out of the terminal building a whole platoon came past at the double, automatic rifles at their sides, boots in concert. They were professionals and the sergeant didn't have to scream.

"Fuckin' army."

I put my overnight bag down and straightened my shoulders as if I were stiff and then I checked. No one I recognized. He was in his mid-twenties and wore a blue padded jacket. He stood half-turned, a fingernail picking at a scab on his cheek. He'd spoken English words to no one in particular.

The army had unrolled barbed wire to sever the approach area and on the far side there were six camouflaged troop transports with canvas sides flapping like drab banners in the wind. Sandbags protected a pair of machine guns. There was a khaki tent with a soldier in front drinking from an enamel mug. A jeep curved round to a gap in the barbed wire and the officer in the front seat showed a pass to the sentries armed with machine-pistols. The jeep passed through and zipped away towards a pre-fabricated portable cabin. A Dutch flag snapped to attention as the officer got down from the jeep and disappeared. I decided that it was the command post that Crevecoeur had been thrown out of to make way for American security.

There was more than army.

The noise came from somewhere over my left shoulder and before I could turn to take them in they'd swept low overhead following the airport perimeter. They banked in a gentle curve that would take them as far as the North Sea.

"Starfighters," the man in the blue padded jacket said. A gust of wind caught him and his hair was all over the place.

"I thought they'd all gone into the ground," I said. It was the Germans who first called the plane the Widowmaker.

He screwed up his eyes to follow the aircraft out of vision. As he turned I took in the badge he wore where a soldier would wear a medal: a clenched fist squeezed out a red drop and on top were the capital letters B.G.O.

"Right," he said, and looked in my eyes a moment.

A whistle shrilled somewhere to the right and I turned as a group of Arabs began walking from a bus towards the entrance to the passenger terminal building. The men carried Kuwait Airways bags and that slow gait that looks as if it has been learned from walking across endless sand. There were two women with only their eyes showing. A man in some airline uniform was counting them.

The whistle blasted again and I noticed a policeman waving an arm above his head. He shouted something and I realized his anger was directed at me and the man with the fly-away hair.

"Fuck them all," he said.

He loped off towards the terminal building.

I picked up my grip and on impulse looked up at the skyline of the building. A khaki figure had me in his binocular sights.

Welcome to Amsterdam.

CHAPTER NINE

"Pig, pig, pig, pig, pig."

They waved their arms and chanted.

It was a schizophrenic crowd. Some had glee on their faces, some were intense with anger.

They had brought a pig into the city centre, a surreal pig with its flanks painted in red and white stripes and big blue stars across its shoulders. It squealed and slithered on the cobbles and darted from one side of the road to the other. My taxi had skirted Leidseplein and been forced to a standstill in a side street by the weight of the crowd. They swirled their arms and shouted in unison, mostly at the animal, at times at the two police who tried to corral it.

"It's because of the peace conference," the taxi-driver said.

"They don't want peace?"

He inspected me in the mirror. His eyes were calm: they had inspected lovers and gamblers and thieves and gawpers and now they saw a fool. He said: "Of course they don't want peace. If there was peace everywhere in the world, they'd have nothing to rebel against." There was certainty in his voice, as if he'd studied philosophy at college. His cigar had gone out and he sucked at it mournfully.

The crowd surged round the taxi and we rocked a bit and then the people parted as the pig dashed forward, seventy or eighty kilos of it, enough to crush a foot that got in the way.

"You know," he said, "half of them will not be meat-eaters because they believe it is cruel, yet they do that to the pig."

He meditated on his cigar and then on my face in the mirror and then on the mob, a hundred, a hundred and fifty of them, it was impossible to estimate in the confines of the side street.

Blocked by the car in the narrow roadway and the crowds on either side, the pig retreated in a lurching run back towards Leidseplein. One of the police made to strike it with his stick and the animal lunged aside, bundling over a thin girl with a crude placard.

The pig vanished, its progress marked by car horns and the screech of tyres. The crowd funnelled after it and we were left with the thin girl on the pavement, rubbing her shin and crying.

The driver engaged gear and edged past the forlorn figure. The placard beside her showed an American flag and the single bold word *ASSASSINS*. Every 'S' had been given a downward stroke to resemble a dollar sign.

As I leaned over the seat to look at the girl and placard, my philosopher-driver said: "She's not hurt. She's only crying because her playmates have gone off and left her. Don't be worried about her."

I wasn't. For the first time I was worrying about myself.

He had looked like a hunter on a mountain ridge and I had been the prey.

My friend Desnos had been murdered, a girl had been abducted, a courier for French Security was being held to ransom, and the moving finger had swung round and pointed at me. For a few instants I had seen the soldier on the rooftop at the airport staring at me through the X12 magnification glasses and if I had stepped out of line he could have switched to following me through the sniperscope of his rifle.

When first you find yourself in the crossed-hairs it changes the colours and shapes of everything around you.

I paid off the taxi and walked the last block to Huidenstraat. A concrete canopy jutted out from the Hotel Excelsior and two sightseeing buses were parked in its shelter. The foyer was like the concourse at a railway station and I paused inside the revolving doors, puzzled.

Poelsma with his large house in a snob district in Paris, another in the south of France, and a third along some tree-shaded canal in this city, a diamond broker, a rich man who employed a nanny and servants, why would he choose to stay in a hotel like this?

"Are you with Thomson Holidays?" His accent was English.

"No, I'm ... "

But he'd already moved on, his hands beseeching another little group.

It was a tiny thing: I realized Poelsma had chosen this hotel because here he was just a room number on an account; nobody paid attention to a face, only a lapel identity tag; here he could come and go unremarked.

Another tiny thing: they had taken such care about my contact at the airport.

Being under the scrutiny of the figure in khaki on the rooftop had touched me, making even tiny things sinister. As indicators they were insignificant and yet they nagged in my mind: normal gangland activities don't stretch to such subtle care.

So I crossed the foyer, carried on past the reception desk and wedged myself into one of the line of phone booths that gave me nearly a hundred and eighty degrees of vision.

"Hotel Excelsior."

"Do you have a Mnr Poelsma staying there?"

"What is his room number, please?"

"That's what I want to know."

"I am sorry, we do not give such information by the telephone."

"Find out his extension. Just connect me to his room."

She sighed, as if doing her job was an imposition. After some seconds, "There is no Mnr Poelsma registered."

She couldn't wait to get off the line.

I'd wanted to walk straight up to have a quiet talk and now Poelsma wasn't even registered. He wouldn't be under an assumed name or I'd have been told. I was at the right hotel because the recognition procedure at the airport had gone precisely according to Sarasini's instructions and the information had come from one of the pals.

The telephone made an irritable little noise at me. I didn't replace the receiver because holding it to my face gave me a reason to be standing there while I tried to settle things in my mind.

It had started with my friend's murder, my sole interest. It had been Crevecoeur who had introduced the question of Poelsma's disappearance. Poelsma, who worked for French Security. Poelsma, whose daughter was spirited away. Poelsma, who might be under duress to do something.

Pressure had been brought on me to help. There had been Crevecoeur's vague threats of deportation and hints of tax investigation, which could mean being kept in custody while the investigation dragged on. In France a dozen people a year commit suicide because of the methods of the tax inspectorate; sometimes *les fiscs* raid a suspect's house before dawn, like the Gestapo.

I didn't understand Poelsma, or the behaviour of Fonza's pals, or the exact relationship between Fonza and Crevecoeur (only Miss Tulloch and Crevecoeur had known of my interest in Poelsma and I couldn't visualize the nanny running to a gang boss; Crevecoeur and Fonza, *copains et coquins*).

Something was eluding me that would make sense out of nonsense. I stood, with the phone still irritable against my ear, and pushed the thing round and tried to make a pattern.

Two of them came in through the revolving door from the street and I registered them automatically, giving no part of my attention to them. I was still thinking about my nonsense and perhaps the facts I was working on weren't the significant ones.

Try again.

My friend Desnos was opening a club and had been killed by thugs from one gang, and did that imply he was pushing drugs for Fonza's gang? It was possible. In France, among the *copains et coquins*, anything was possible. A security outfit might decide that pushing drugs was the best way to get a bigger budget; one of the French outfits had been uncovered in the United States doing just that. So what would that make Poelsma?

I shook my head, stuffed with cotton wool.

The two who'd come in through the revolving door were police. They weren't in uniform but there was no mistaking them. They were checking faces as they moved to the reception desk.

Try the other angle. The kidnappers gave every appearance of knowing Poelsma. Could he be the drug-pusher? Perhaps they were no more than heads who were desperate…

The irritable noise stopped as I replaced the phone on the cradle.

It was because of the police. Another tiny indication nudged my brain.

One cop was running a finger down the register; the other was still skimming across faces, including mine, and the little group of men and women who came down the stairs. They were looking for somebody; maybe a request had gone through Interpol for Poelsma to be located. No, because the cop had spent four or five seconds checking my features against a memory-bank of faces. And now they were questioning the reception clerk. One of them lit a cigarette and then they left.

I had no more facts. Instead I had more doubts set up by the police checking out the hotel, the security effort inside the terminal building, the machine-gun posts, the sharpshooter on the roof, the Starfighters doing a sweep.

I chose my moment and walked across to the front desk. There was a fan of Dutch, French, German and English newspapers. They all carried big headlines about the Summit conference that was to start in Amsterdam in three days.

The police had left the register on the counter and there was nothing on the open page. The clerk was dealing with a blue-rinse woman who wouldn't let go of his sleeve, but he had an eye on me as I turned back a page and then another and then I found Poelsma, registered on the 20th, account settled the 22nd, and so the switchboard girl had been correct if unhelpful, and then the clerk broke away and came and got his hands on the register. There were furrows of displeasure on his forehead because they don't like you seeing the names and the room numbers.

"I was supposed to meet a friend here," I told him.

"It is against the policy … " he began.

"Mnr Poelsma," I said.

He glanced at the register. "Mnr Poelsma checked out after breakfast this morning."

"Yes, he said he might have to leave but he would give a forwarding address."

"Just a minute." He disappeared through a frosted-glass door and returned after half a minute. "Mnr Poelsma left no forwarding address."

I'd been inside the Excelsior no more than twenty minutes but in Holland that's time enough for clouds to rear up. The rain slanted down, gusted by the wind, and already the cyclists wore capes that covered their knees.

I turned left, in towards the city centre, and stopped on a bridge.

I could answer the first question: why had Poelsma chosen to come to Amsterdam? Answer: because he knew that was where the kidnappers had brought his daughter.

But the second question: why had the kidnappers chosen to come to Amsterdam?

I stared down at the canal, its surface pockmarked by rain.

CHAPTER TEN

AMSTERDAM
THURSDAY 22 MARCH
4.40 P.M.

I knocked at the door and thought I caught a movement in the room beyond.

"*Oui*?" The voice was close, but against the solid wall next to the doorframe rather than the flimsy protection of the wooden panels.

"It's Cody."

"Push your passport under the door."

Even when he opened the door he held the knife in the throwing stance in case I had been acting with a muzzle at the back of my neck. Sarasini took his role as forward scout for Fonza very seriously.

"Poelsma is no longer at his hotel. He checked out."

The Corsican dialect is a curious one but you didn't need to understand it to know he was cursing. It came in a soft mumble, to himself.

"I had a meeting with the pals at lunch, on the *capo*'s business, and they didn't tell me. Nobody double-crosses the *capo*."

"It's not that. They'd traced where Poelsma was; perhaps no one said to put a watchman on him."

His pink tongue came out and tasted the stale air of his hotel room. Poelsma's disappearance was a personal affront to the second most important man in Paris.

"He's not turned up at his house," I said. I'd looked up the address in the telephone directory. It was a patrician building, an eighteenth-century merchant's house, mellowed brick, with a huge hook under the eaves for hauling the bulkier items of furniture to the upper rooms. A sort of caretaker had answered the door. The *mynheer* was absent, abroad. I'd told him it was urgent and I'd received the Paris address. The old caretaker was slow-moving and had the aura of somebody who habitually told the truth. I'd watched for an hour anyway and there was no movement across any of the windows.

Sarasini was angry. He grew still angrier when I told him I was having nothing more to do with him, Fonza or their pals.

He said: "What do you mean? I have the *capo*'s orders."

"Your pals turned up one lead and it's broken. I don't want to be tied down."

"What are you going to do?"

I wouldn't tell him and suddenly the knife glinted in his hand again. We kept our silence while he sighted down the length of the blade against one of the lamps, a gleam of light dancing across his eyes, and tested the point on the ball of his thumb.

He was no brain, all nerves, and it worried me. A knife-artist should be full of confidence, but he lived in a world where virility was measured in the length of your gun barrel. His insecurity constantly flickered on the surface and I had to build him up.

"You like the knife, don't you," I said. "It's better than a gun."

He looked at me. His tongue was searching, searching, and then it slipped back in his mouth. He made a noise in his throat.

He said: "It's quieter than a pistol and it holds more surprises." He bent and stretched his right arm, easing the elbow joint I had kicked the previous night. "Understand what I'm getting at?" He picked up a cushion and plumped it with his fist. "Imagine this cushion is a man."

He walked across the room, dropped the cushion out of sight behind the bed and crossed back to the dressing table, crouching in its shelter. I was standing to one side by the door and his eyes flicked at me.

"Here: one man, one knife, one throw. Over there: one man, one pistol, six shots, possibly eight. It is stalemate, each hidden from the other, neither wanting to risk a move that might expose. Perhaps you think the odds favour the gunman because he can use his pistol to keep my head below the level of the dressing table while he crawls to a commanding position."

I kept quiet but my whole attention was on him, wanting him to soak in how riveting I found him.

He concentrated on me and his stare was shaded with a slight smile. He held the stage and it pleased him. I waited. Perhaps half a second before he made his move his eyes lost their focus on me. Then he turned his head and raised his hand and still in the crouched position behind the dressing table he threw. It was an upwards-slanting throw, following through so that in the end-position his arm gave a Nazi-style salute. He made use of the ceiling but it wasn't just a question of knowing the exact spot to bisect the angle and give the correct rebound. He wasn't throwing a spherical object but a spinning knife with a sharp and a blunt end. He had to hit the ceiling with one hundred per cent precision when the spin was bringing the handle in a forward arc. Any error and the tip of the knife would dig into the ceiling at the point of impact. The knife's flight was abruptly deflected and it dropped in the lee of the bed. He rose to his feet and crossed the room and picked up the cushion. The blade was imbedded. It was the sort of party trick that professional throwers might perfect, like placing knives skin-close round a revolving body. But it had importance for him.

"*Au poil,*" I said, putting admiration into my voice.

Sarasini made a little guttural noise of pleasure.

He checked my face and then he turned his attention to the knife, going through the ritual with the point and the alignment of the blade.

"You can't do that with the heavy knives," he said. "The balance and the flighting may be perfect but with anything above about 230 grams the momentum is too great and you end up with a skid mark on the ceiling."

He looked much easier with me now but I boosted him again. "What happens if you're against two gunmen?"

He stared, the faint smile drifting into his eyes and out again. He jabbed the knife in the direction of the electric flex running down the wall from the switch by the door.

"At night: I throw and fuse the lights: then I move quietly in the dark and take them one by one with my hands. During the day: I drop the first gunman, as I showed. The second gunman can't be certain how many blades I have so I talk him into surrender. Of course, he could be a hero bent on suicide but there aren't too many of those. Otherwise there wouldn't be a president alive in Europe."

The knife slipped up the sleeve of his jacket and while the smile still hovered near his lips I said: "The *capo* has a good man."

His reaction was fierce. He stood in front of me, face thrust forward into mine. "I would do anything for the *capo,* anything. Kill a man," he ran his finger across his throat, "go to my own death, anything. He comes from the same village as I do in Corsica, up in the mountains near Corte. Do you know the island?"

I shook my head.

"At Corte we are cursed with the Foreign Legion. They have a camp nearby where the discipline is very harsh. If a soldier does something wrong they make him clean the parade ground on his hands and knees, picking up leaves and stones with his teeth, licking the steps with his tongue. The men are Germans and Poles and Finns and they are no better than animals. When camp life breaks them, they desert. We had one in our village, an animal from Bulgaria. He came after dark and ripped the dress off my sister's back as she walked home from our cousin's farm. It was the *capo,* though he wasn't *capo* then, who heard her screams and he killed the brute with these."

He held up his hands, fingers rigid.

"I helped the *capo* bury the brute, out in the pine forest, but we knew it would be no good. They track the deserters with helicopters in the air and dogs on the ground and they'd find the body eventually. I went away with the *capo* before dawn down to Bastia and the boat across to France. I was seventeen."

His tongue came out and for once he seemed angered by it, found its lack of control humiliating. I don't think he noticed it normally. He put his knuckles to his cheeks and turned aside.

I spoke quietly to him. "I think you should go and see your pals again, see if they can turn up a fresh lead."

He nodded, frowning. "How about you?"

"Will your pals be easy with a woman present?"

He shook his head.

"Then come back and tell me."

I gave him ten minutes start before I left the hotel.

CHAPTER ELEVEN

I began west of Rembrantsplein for no better reason than the three who'd run off with nine-year-old Simone had been young, and if you were young and had long hair you'd pass completely unnoticed around Leidseplein, Rembrandtsplein and Zeedijk.

I'd waited until darkness because I wasn't going to do the rounds twice and a lot of the places put up their shutters during the daylight hours. The clouds hung low, fat with rain, dirty with the glow off the city. There was a sheen of dampness on the streets and the shadows of people walking broke the reflections from garish neon. Porno, Blue Movies, Non-stop Striptease, Live Acts—the English words throbbed with promise.

On one wall, more English words: *The dawn is red. BGO.*

It was mainly instinct I was following, a little logic mixed in.

The three kidnappers had given the appearance of knowing Poelsma and had disappeared and by the end of the next day Poelsma had left Paris and flown to Amsterdam. He had avoided his house, stayed at a hotel. Inference: he knew the kidnappers were based in Amsterdam and had felt it important to stay incognito until he'd made contact. He would have checked his daughter was alive and what the kidnappers demands were. Then he'd got out.

"He's a friend. Have you seen him?"

"Never."

Poelsma had moved into the Excelsior on Tuesday, spent two nights there, left this morning. Inference: what he'd been asked to do took some time to set up.

I tried again. The sign said: Krazy Kitty—Topless downstairs, Bottomless upstairs.

"It's a friend I'm looking for. Do you recognize him?"

"Never seen him."

"Would you remember?"

"If he was dressed like that, *ja*."

The barman showed it to a plump girl on a stool and they both laughed, her flesh shaking in the glow from the pink shaded light.

"Do you think upstairs … ?"

"So, you like looking at the girls too," the barman said, and the pink jelly shook with laughter again.

All I had to help were the photos Crevecoeur had handed me. The one of Poelsma was a formal portrait and showed a man with dark curly hair, clean shaven, wearing a sober suit and conservative tie. The one of the daughter showed a dark-eyed sensitive face and long dark ringlets.

"She won't look like that now," Crevecoeur had said. "But if they've taken the kitchen scissors to her hair she'll be very noticeable."

I turned the corner as a man got off his bicycle and leaned it carefully against a lamp post. He looked up and down the street and took out an aerosol can and sprayed on the brick: *The future is red.* The aerosol artist inspected me and turned back to the wall. He added as a signature: *BGO.*

It wasn't the girl's photo I showed in bars, it was the one of Poelsma. The kidnappers would be certain not to give him the address where they held Simone, they'd just let him talk to her on the phone.

Papa, you must do as they ask, whatever it is, or they say I shan't see you again.

And then Poelsma would ask what it was they wanted him to do and they'd let his little girl tell him: because if one of the kidnap gang told him, his reaction would be anger and he'd want to fight; but if his own daughter told him, he'd want to protect her by agreeing.

I had a hunch Poelsma would have insisted on a meeting.

"Have you seen ... "

"*Wacht even, ik begrijp 't niet. Jan, sprecht U Engels?*"

"*Ik ken een beetjie. Wat wenst U?*"

"*Nee, dat meisje.*"

"Okay, sugar, what are you looking for?"

"My friend. I was supposed to meet him in a bar but I lost the address."

He shook his head.

"Perhaps your colleague ... ?"

The other one looked and shook in turn.

They would arrange an rdv, a neutral place, where they could talk. A café or bar was obvious. Or a station platform. Or a canal boat. Or the Rijksmuseum. But start with the bars.

Even if they hadn't rendezvoused in a bar, it was likely that Poelsma had been seen around in the past. He knew the kidnappers, and not from the diamond-broking business.

The place was called Lippenstift. I had to pass a black bouncer with a black Alsatian on a chain. The room was half full and several people turned to stare. I was the only woman.

The young man in a black leather jerkin said: "He looks very straight. Try the Vroom-Vroom across the road."

There was quite a lot more noise coming from doorways now, jukeboxes spewing out the same sounds they do in all cities. A drunk wanted me to go down an alley and followed when I ignored his urgent hiss. I let him get close enough to put a hand on me and kicked back with my heel at his instep.

It was after eleven and I had swung round three sides of the square and the complex of streets towards the canal. Concorde, negative. Running Dog, negative. Oom Paul, negative. Wet Pussy, negative.

More paint dripped down a wall: *Blood is red. BGO.*

The final reason I trusted in a bar was that Fonza's pals knew about Poelsma's presence in Amsterdam. He'd been seen around, perhaps he was a customer of theirs.

Two or three kids brushed past me, their shoes high in the air as they ran, and, as the sound of the police siren rose at my back, one turned a face that flashed watercress-green in the light from a neon sign, and then they'd disappeared between parked cars and past a cluster of people round a man playing a guitar and mouth organ and cymbals.

The sign said Snelboom and the window was blocked out with posters for Bols and Bokma and Johnnie Walker and Breda.

"Yes, two or three nights ago."

"Are you sure?"

"Yes, I'm sure." He leaned his knuckles on the bar to stare at me and there was no humour in his eyes. "You're a friend?"

"Not exactly. I was supposed to pass on a message for a friend."

"Well, he's not here now."

Some are places for making a friend for the night. Some are places for an illusion of companionship. Some are places to show you are incapable of shock. Some are places to spend money because that is how you know you are enjoying yourself. This was a place to get a hangover. There were four men at a table, Polish seamen at a guess, and they were raucous. A woman stood by their table and one of the seamen had a hand up her pleated skirt and when she laughed her mouth was a red gash across an empy white landscape. The barman picked up a bottle of *jenever* and went to the end of the bar where a solitary brooded over an empty glass. He returned.

"Are you drinking or just asking questions?"

"I'll have the same. You?"

He poured one glass. I gave him twenty guilders and got no change.

There was a rowdy burst of singing from the seamen but the barman looked the other way towards the street and when the singing broke down in confusion I heard the noise, the police siren. It was stationary a block or two away.

"They're wasting their damn time." He looked back at me. "If they've left their car it's because the ones they want have vanished through some door, and by now they're in a closet in an upper room, or buried in a cellar, or out through the back door."

I picked the photo off the counter and tucked it in my shoulder-bag. "The man's name is Poelsma. Do you know him?"

He shook his head. His face was solid, a peasant's, with pale bushy eyebrows. At some point he'd met a bottle and it hadn't been patched neatly. The old scar had a double row of stitchmarks along the jaw, as if he'd been built like Frankenstein.

"But you're still certain?"

"I'm sure. I'll tell you why I'm sure." There was a certain heat in his voice. "He came in early in the afternoon looking like a bloody businessman from Frankfurt or Zurich. But his Dutch was Amsterdamer and he went straight to that table by the door to the toilet. There was a woman at the table. He didn't shake hands but he seemed to know her, leaning over the table while she spoke. I took him a beer but he wasn't drunk. I had two youngsters here at the bar and they wanted addresses so I wasn't paying your friend any attention. But he'd been here perhaps ten minutes when he got up and I could see he was all wrong. His face, you know, like a bad face in the mirror in the morning, very white, and the eyes round and black. He came towards the bar and then he vomited down the backs of the two youngsters. That's how I'm sure of him."

The door opened and a policeman was inside with his hand loosening the pistol in his holster and there was another in the street behind him. I heard the hoo-ha louder through the open door. It hadn't moved.

The cop's eyes went round the drinkers in the room and he asked the barman a question and then we were on our own again.

"Who are they looking for?"

"I don't know," he said. "BGO maybe."

"Who are BGO?"

"Nobody."

There was shouting from the seamen and he looked at their table, gauging how much more drink they could take before he lost his profit in broken furniture. The woman was sitting on the knees of the tall thin one, running her fingers through his hair.

"Had you seen this girl before, the one Poelsma spoke to?"

"I hadn't seen her before."

"Or Poelsma?"

"I haven't seen Poelsma. I haven't seen the girl. I haven't seen who the cops are chasing. I haven't seen you."

He picked my glass off the counter, drank it and turned his back on me to wash it in the sink.

The stitchmarks down his jawline pulsed.

Outside the police klaxon was switched off. It would take a chair across the skull to switch off the seamen.

CHAPTER TWELVE

AMSTERDAM
FRIDAY 23 MARCH
1.15 A.M.

I stood back in the doorway not because the shadow was friendly but for protection from the rain. I waited for him, uneasy because his voice had stumbled with excitement.

A man came past with a large black umbrella shielding his face from the gusting rain; he had an anonymous dog that tugged its lead at every tree. A taxi, cruising slowly. A boy and girl on their way to bed.

A police car slid through the night and stopped opposite me. There was only the road's width between us and I could easily have crossed. I could just imagine their response.

"Goeden avond, Juffrouw, hoe gaat 't?"

"I need your help."

"What is the matter?"

"A young girl has been kidnapped."

"Your daughter?"

"No, somebody I've never met."

"I see. When did this take place?"

"Sunday morning."

"Five days ago? Where?"

"In Paris."

"Then surely it is the business of the French authorities?"

"The girl has been brought to Amsterdam."

"But we have heard nothing through Interpol."

"No, it's my instinct that tells me."

"A woman's intuition, Juffrouw?"

"Something more than that."

"Why have the parents not reported this serious crime to the police?"

"Because the father is being blackmailed to do something."

"You have evidence?"

"Not strictly."

"What is his name?"

"Theo Poelsma."

"The boss of the *Diamant-firma?*"

"He works for French Security as a courier."

"Come, come, Juffrouw, he is a highly respected *burger.* How do you know?"

"A Chief Inspector in the Sûreté Nationale told me."

"Is that a fact? What is his name?"

"Crevecoeur."

"But Chief Inspector Crevecoeur was in Amsterdam on Wednesday in conference with the security branch of the Koninklijke Marechaussee. He never requested co-operation in this matter. What is your name, Juffrouw? Show us your papers. What is your interest in this charade? Have you been drinking? Kindly accompany us to Elandsgracht."

They were sizing me up through the window of the car. When the neon sign flashed *AMSTEL* I lost their faces behind the reflection on the glass. When the sign cut out I saw their eyes steady. One of them used a thin cheroot. Their mouths smiled at some joke and the car eased away, a puff of grey exhaust smoke spiralling behind in the damp air.

He was ten minutes late.

I was positive it was his car from the way it cruised close to the kerb, slowing, accelerating, slowing while he peered into shadows and I stepped out of the doorway to the edge of the sidewalk so he'd see me. He flashed the heads and gunned the motor and had to brake noisily.

Sarasini was on edge because Fonza had issued explicit instructions and yet I had simply walked away during the afternoon. He leaned across the seat and punched at the handle of the door.

"Come on, get in." The voice was rasping.

He'd hired a BMW three litre and I thought that was typical of him, needing the reassurance of power in his hands.

"Hurry," he said.

Sarasini spoke French to me and he'd dropped into familiar *tutoiement*. He'd shown abruptness and anger at me on the phone, but now we were linked together carrying out his boss's instructions. I had become a *copine*.

We left some rubber on the road and I said: "There's a squad car prowling, so if it's truly urgent don't attract their attention."

We crossed Rokin a couple of seconds after the lights had blinked red and cut across the bows of several cars and taxis. The lights switch from red to green without passing through amber and Dutch traffic is usually lethargic in getting away; but at that time of night everyone is impatient and we were lucky not to clip the frontrunners in the surge.

"Jesus, Sarasini." I looked at him and he was frowning, his tongue desperate to escape his mouth. The whiteness of his knuckles on the wheel showed in the glow from the dashboard.

The whole car rattled over the paving and I thought he'd bite through his tongue.

We took a right and then a left over a canal and were heading down Leidsestraat on the route that leads to the airport and southwest beyond that down to The Hague and the sea.

"Tell me what it is."

I had telephoned him because he might have turned up something useful when he met his pals. Also in the back of my mind was the suspicion that the barman at the Snelboom wasn't being as helpful as he might and a visit from the pals might loosen him. Sarasini wouldn't speak on the phone. No time, he said.

His face was bathed in cold orange from the overhead street lighting, his tongue like a questing grey slug.

"On Tuesday evening Poelsma called one of our pals here and wanted to arrange a deal. Poelsma wanted guns, not pistols or shotguns; he wanted sub-machine guns, Schmeissers or Uzis, cleaned up, in working order. He wanted six, and for each gun he wanted six magazines of ammunition. You must realize that Holland still lives in the Dark Ages and for stuff like that it would be necessary to go to Germany or Belgium. Everything was to be done in a great hurry. It was secret, naturally, but it was the urgency that came across."

We were pushing south of the city through a suburb of apartment blocks that could have been anywhere on the peripheral road round Paris, the service lights in the staircases shining, skeletons in the night.

"There's no doubt about this? Your pal can be relied on?"

"Willy de Groot. He's done a lot of deals with the *capo*. Two-way business. One pal never lets another pal down."

"But he lets Poelsma down? He's told you about it."

"Poelsma isn't a pal. Poelsma is a customer."

He turned his wrist, trying to read the dial.

"It's ten to two," I told him.

Sarasini grunted. The tension was still in the set of his shoulders and the hands on the wheel.

"It's arranged for two o'clock. Willy's already been paid and he's going to complete the contract. They're Schmeissers and Willy said he had to go all the way to Aachen to locate them and then there was some fuss about agreeing the drop-point. Poelsma's out of it and Willy's been talking with someone else who's very edgy."

"What's our plan?"

"There was no time for a plan. Willy is just doing the *capo* a favour. He hands over the merchandise, so he's completed his side of the contract. If we observe the delivery, or appear after Willy has gone, that's okay. He's glad to be of service. I think he owes the *capo* one anyhow."

It's called honour among thieves.

Muck was coming on to the windscreen from the nightrider in front. It had a dozen red and orange lights on its tail, a Bilbao licence and a TIR plate. We took the truck, buffeting in its slipstream, and Sarasini braked suddenly and we cut in front of the sixteen-wheeler as the sign to the airport came up. The inside of the car was flooded in sudden daylight and there was hissing like an old steam locomotive and then dark returned as we peeled away into the turn-off.

The sound of a foghorn howled away into the night. I kept silence. Sarasini's tongue was too busy to talk.

The airport was on our right. Police cars had angled into the approach road and floodlighting bathed the area. Clusters of men in uniform stood by red and white striped barriers with nothing to do in the dead hours before daylight.

I checked my watch again but didn't tell Sarasini because he was pushing his luck with the car already and I had no wish to end the night in the cold room with an identity tag round my big toe.

We looked to be running into suburbs again. A sign came up that said Amstelveen.

Sarasini said: "A couple of kilometres on the right."

I asked: "Have you been there before?"

"No. Following Willy's instructions."

The turn-off was down a road to Uithoorn. The land lay flat on either side, the fields bare, dark shapes of houses and farms, spikes of poplars.

Sarasini slowed right down, switched off both pairs of iodine heads, coasted until his eyes began to adjust to the light conditions. The sky was eight-tenths cloud, a few stars showing in a break to the right, the road a shade lighter grey than the fields.

"Good," he said.

We pulled off the road, across the cycle-track, and into the shelter of a stack of drainage pipes. Above the car were the high wires of pylons that marched away to the horizon. I checked and said to him: "It's eight after."

He switched off the ignition and wound down his window.

I noticed the sound of distant traffic on the main road, the ticking of the engine as it cooled, a faint hum from the wires overhead.

He said: "The track is about a hundred metres ahead on the left, running down towards a river or a drainage canal. There's supposed to be a barn or a farm building of some kind. That's where Willy is making the delivery. We'll follow the other car as it goes."

"They could have taken the stuff from him and be on their way already. We're late."

We stared to the left where the denseness showed us the position of the building. It was impossible to make out a car or anybody waiting.

"No," he said. "We're in time. If the delivery had already been made, we'd have met Willy on the road."

He cracked the knuckles of one of his hands and then said: "Schmeissers, that's a real cow. What do they want Schmeissers for?"

Everybody still talks about Schmeissers though Schmeisser only designed one SMG and that was back in the First World War. They would most likely be 9 mm Walther sub-machine guns, because they're in use with the West German police and they could have got "lost" from the headquarters in Aachen. I remembered the magazine held something like thirty-two rounds and they'd wanted six magazines for each weapon. They were planning for war.

Sarasini began on the knuckles of his other hand.

The ribbon of tarmac went straight for quite a way before it curved out of view. There were the stationary lights of a village some distance in front, and moving pencils of light to the left on a road near the horizon.

That's where the noise came from. I couldn't place it at first because I had my window down and was concentrating on the grey ribbon that stretched to the front.

The wind blowing in from the west was against the approaching noise or we'd have caught it before it was in sight. As it was we suddenly saw lights close by, red and white winking, as it followed the guide-line of the electricity pylons. The sound swelled into a clatter and then it hovered above the barn. Landing lights came on and we could plainly discern the curved corrugated roof of the building, the big car parked beside it and a solitary figure standing with an arm thrown across his face against the brightness from the sky.

"*Ah putain, putain, putain.*" It was spoken under his breath.

The helicopter sank down on the short grass of the meadow and the landing lights faded out.

CHAPTER THIRTEEN

UITHOORN ROAD
FRIDAY 23 MARCH
2.20 A.M.

He had the knife out.

I hadn't seen any movement but the shaft was in the palm of his hand and his thumb played over the edge of the steel. He had lost the strength of the BMW to the superior power of the helicopter and now he retreated to his knife to draw comfort.

They hadn't killed the engine of the helicopter so we were unable to pick out voices but we could see figures. Somebody had a flashlamp and it illuminated a face and bobbed across the grass between the helicopter and the car. The beam of the lamp danced around checking for ambush cover, and then the person holding it disappeared inside the double doors of the barn. The lamp reappeared and I thought at least two of them had come and possibly there was still a third in the pilot's seat.

Sarasini had his hand on the car door and I reached out to him.

"Even if you took those ones, that wouldn't be good enough. We don't know where their base is, where they're holding the child, where Poelsma has gone. If they asked for six machine pistols, there'll be more of them."

"I'll ram the *bat-oeufs*."

I didn't argue. The same reasoning applied to the helicopter as to them, and after some seconds he worked it out and sat back.

In the beam from the flashlamp I saw the tailgate of the car lift up. The car was big, square-ended, a Volvo station wagon or similar. The light became confused in the movement of bodies.

"Your pal, did he go alone?"

"That was one of the conditions."

"Did he agree?"

Sarasini agonized to himself, not replying.

"Is there a map in the car?"

He opened the glove compartment. There was a map and I couldn't read it in the darkness and the overhead light was too big a risk.

"Do you smoke?"

"No."

"No matches?"

"I've got this."

He had a pencil-torch, useful for finding the keyhole.

It was a Shell map, the sort hire cars have, the big routes marked and the towns and the canals and lakes. Even the road we were on, stretching south. It didn't mark the row of pylons.

Two of the figures lugged boxes between them to the waiting helicopter. Their shadows loomed on its side, fuzzy and grotesque from the flashlamp left on the ground beside the car.

Above our heads the power lines looped from pylon to pylon and I tried to calculate the directions: straight across my right shoulder, bisecting the road at virtually forty-five degrees, and disappearing into the darkness half-left. On the map that gave the direction as south-east and the nearest large town in that direction was Utrecht.

The helicopter would need somewhere isolated to put down or they'd have the neighbours parting the bedroom curtains. They'd been following the pylons as markers and the inference was their base was before Utrecht. I didn't care to imagine it was the far side of Utrecht because we'd be lost. Even so our chance of success had an appallingly low probability but there was no better plan.

"What are you thinking?" he asked.

He'd tucked the blade away up his sleeve and was looking in my direction. It crossed my mind that he'd shifted his dependence from the knife to me.

"I don't know how they got hold of the helicopter," I told him. "Or why they need it. I mean, they wouldn't want it just to pick up this consignment. Something bigger. It's the middle of the night so we assume they're going back to their base. That's where we have to go."

"The BMW can't fly."

"No," I agreed. I left it at that. There didn't seem any point in telling him how he was going to have to drive.

Headlights approached down the road from Uithoorn. Over by the barn there was a sudden scurry of activity. In the lamplight I saw one of the figures had broken open a box and was holding a Schmeisser, and then the light was doused.

The motor of the helicopter still clattered because they didn't want to lose any time in lifting off after they'd loaded. We couldn't hear the car until it was almost on us, the noise of the helicopter engine drowning its approach. Over by the barn they would hear nothing, just see its headlights. The car passed and I watched the red tail lights dwindle in the distance.

"Come on," I said, "switch on."

Then it happened. I was unprepared and the shock hit me like a fist under the ribs.

Across the meadow the flashlamp flicked on again and its beam swept round until it locked on a figure standing by the rear left wheel of the station wagon. Willy de Groot. At this distance he had no face, he was just someone in a hat and raincoat, and he lifted an arm to blot out the glare from his eyes. I thought I could make out one other figure moving over there and then I saw quick stabs of light and picked up the staccato chatter through the helicopter noise and the man called Willy de Groot was flung back against the car, his hat spinning into the night. He clawed at his chest and there seemed something dark there but it could just have been the scrabbling shadows of his fingers. He toppled sideways and the beam from the flashlamp followed him to the ground. There were more stabs of light and rapid-fire explosions. His body jerked as the Schmeisser's bullets hammered it.

It seemed to carry on for ever, the whole magazine I felt, an insane, vitriolic, hate-filled action.

The body lay still. Somebody approached and prodded it with a shoe.

"*Les salauds. On l'a fait couic.*"

Sarasini made a noise in his throat and the knife was in his hand again.

"Don't. You can do nothing for him."

The emotions ploughed across his face.

"He's a pal. The *capo* never …"

"Shit. Can't you understand? We're not in the *maquis* in Corsica, we're two hundred and fifty metres away across open land. You have your knife and they have a helicopter and six sub-machine guns. Start the engine."

Over by the barn they were packing the body of Sarasini's pal into the back of the car.

"All they'll hear is the helicopter. Just don't switch on the lights until we're well away."

I found my seat belt and the clip was slippery between my fingers. I hoped there was no sweat on Sarasini's hands. He still hesitated.

"If they get a head start," I said, "we'll be hopelessly lost."

Sarasini turned the key, got into gear and moved back on to the tarmac ribbon.

"Go on," I urged. "This is the best chance. Their eyes will be on the body not on the road."

CHAPTER FOURTEEN

UITHOORN/LOOSDRECHTSCHE PLASSEN
FRIDAY 23 MARCH
2.35 A.M.

N o need to urge him faster.

He was hunched forward peering out at the ribbon stretching away in front and snapping up through second and third, toeing the accelerator to the floorboards.

The BMW was his source of strength and when the helicopter had appeared out of the night his strength had been emasculated. Now he was given the chance to regain it, to prove his virility in a straight contest, hunting down the cause of his lost manhood. Regaining something that has been lost is powerful motivation and his brain and reflexes and nerves were responding.

The engine revs were high as he pulled the gear-stick into top.

Our initial course lay south.

After a couple of kilometres Sarasini switched on the lights.

Then the road took a gentle bend and he switched to full beam.

The trouble was the row of pylons angled away south-east and once the helicopter got going it would travel rapidly away from our line.

I was leaning over the back of the bucket seat to keep watch through the window behind and I thought I saw winking lights rise in the distance. I closed my eyes and opened them again, focussing slightly to one side to avoid the central blind spot of night vision. There they were. It had begun.

The airborne lights gained height and started moving away to the west. If they went west, they weren't returning the way they'd come and my flimsy reasoning was blown to the wind.

"Jesus, where are they going?"

Sarasini was trying to look in the mirror and keep driving and there was a rough patch as we strayed too far to the right, throwing grit against the side panels.

"Bloody drive," I yelled. Churning inside, I had strayed into English but he understood well enough.

The lights of the helicopter swung in an arc and it had just been a positioning move and now the lights were on an easterly course. I lost them for a good ten seconds as they traversed the car's bodywork by the rear window. They reappeared very faint as the seat belt bit into my chest, and there was the noise of the tyres ripping off rubber on the surface of the road, and I twisted frontwards as Sarasini put the car down to third. The lamps gleamed on the sign for a minor road crossing.

"That road's not marked on the map," I shouted against the racing of the gear and the scream of the tyres. "Go on to Uithoorn."

"We'll lose them."

"It's only another kilometre."

He ignored me. The pull of the helicopter was stronger than my objection.

He took the turn too fast and the back end was yawing as he corrected the line and his foot was already dropping hard on the accelerator. We were on to a minor road with white-painted wooden fencing on the right and a drainage ditch on the left. I had the map spread on my knees and his pencil-flashlight in my hand and there was nothing marked where we were.

Shapes flickered past the glass and I glanced up at stark poplars; and then there was a rise and bump as we hit the bridge and we were over the Amstel River, dark and straight.

"Can you see it?" He was flicking his head away to the left and back front again. "I've lost the bastard."

I thought it was because his eyes were adapted to the light conditions of the road in full beam and couldn't adjust to the darker sky. I peered beyond him where the helicopter should be and there was a confusion of bright pinpoints in the heavens, the Plough, Ursa Major, Ursa Minor, shining in a break in the clouds. No moving identification lights stood out.

"Switch off the heads."

We hurtled ahead in sudden blackness and if we'd met a bend in the road we'd have been bowled over by the impact of the drainage ditch and sent spinning across the meadow in a series of rolls with the car falling apart around us and the fuel tank splitting, and even if we were conscious when the car jolted to a stop the doors would have buckled and in the sudden onrush of flame we'd hammer uselessly to get away.

I studied through the window. I could see nothing, no helicopter, no line of pylons, there were a dozen black and white cows in the meadow, then nothing.

"Switch on."

Sarasini was braking again and up front there was a junction and I told him: "Go right."

"But they're left."

"If they're heading in the direction of Utrecht they'll have to pass in front of us. Go right, and left at the main road."

We turned on to the highway and there were headlamps bright behind us and then fading as we rushed through a strung-out village. Ahead across the flat landscape was a necklace of lights where the autoroute went south-east, skirting Utrecht and on to Eindhoven and towards the German border, and the bloody thing passed right over us.

We both caught the clatter above our windrush and engine noise.

First I saw the pylons with their feet in a shallow lake marching from left to right and then the winking lights suddenly reappeared as the helicopter left the clear patch in the sky and passed against the backdrop of cloud again. It was hard to estimate its height, a hundred metres, a little more. The pilot could go no higher because he was navigating on the line of pylons and starlight was little help.

"We're okay."

I had never had a clear sight of it but if it were an Alouette or a Bell Jet Ranger its cruise speed would be in the 180 to 215 kph bracket. The BMW had a theoretical plus over the Alouette but the Jet Ranger could outpace it even in optimum conditions. At night, whatever helicopter it was, it had the advantage of a clear line of flight and no obstacles.

We passed two cars stopped on the verge, their doors open and interior lights glowing. Four figures stood in a little group.

"Do they have friends out?" he asked.

"Why should they? They don't know about us. They're not expecting anyone in a car."

It would be a different matter when the helicopter sank to earth. They had the Schmeissers, or whatever models they were, and they were killers.

The BMW peeled off to the right on the slip road and we joined the E9 nudging 90 kph with Sarasini surging it up through third to pull away in front of a refrigerated meat transporter.

The autoroute was broad and straight, very sparse traffic, and Sarasini kept his foot flat on the floor. The speedo notched 190, 195 and hovered under 200. I leaned over and found the wiper switch, and the blades swept aside the muck thrown on the windscreen.

I picked up the line of pylons again over to the left, skirting the shore of another lake, and I couldn't be certain whether I'd picked out the tail and cockpit lights because there was a dirty glow on the cloud base. I checked the map and the outlying districts of Utrecht were half a dozen kilometres away.

"We've got to get off to the left."

It was over a minute on the autoroute before the next exit came up and we had to swing right round and up and over before we were headed east.

We crossed railroad tracks and a canal and were into a small town with a name beginning with M. Ahead was a junction and we needed to choose, left or right.

Sarasini brought the car to a halt. I wound down the window to look and listen. The sky was empty. The drizzle had set ir again and there was cold damp on my face.

I flicked the flashlight over the map and traced with my finger. "We're about here. If we turn right we're running into Utrecht and unless they're overflying to some spot between Utrecht and the German border that's no use."

He didn't look at the map. It was the car and the night world outside that claimed him. He was staring into the shadows beyond a parked pick-up, his breathing shallow and quick. He spoke without turning.

"They've got the helicopter. Why not carry on to Germany?"

"They made contact in Amsterdam. They won't be based out of the country."

He was in gear before I'd finished the sentence, and put full lock on the wheel at the junction and we were heading north through the darkened village.

Not everyone was asleep. Sarasini threw us up through the gears and we were over 120 kph when we reached a run of small houses at the fringe of the village. They had diminutive square gardens and young conifers and clipped hedges. A light shone over a carport and I don't know whether it was the garage light that confused him or whether he saw us coming but misjudged Sarasini's brutal acceleration.

The VW edged out of the drive-in and attempted to dart across the road in front of us. Sarasini hit the brake and then the BMW was drifting sideways on the greasy surface as he pulled down on his right hand, with the tyres losing their grip and the beam of our lights sweeping across neat gardens and the howl of the rubber in our ears. He lifted his foot off the pedal and the tyres stopped the skid, gaining traction, and he pumped at the brakes again. There was still the squeal of rubber as centrifugal force fought against the angle of the front wheels. We swung round the sloping rear end of the Beetle and Sarasini straightened the line of the car. Three seconds, four seconds in all. I registered the other driver's mouth open in an unheard scream and his ghost-white hand raised. It was sheer animal reaction, as though a hand could protect his face from an impact with 1400 kilos of metal.

"*Espèce de con.*" Sarasini's tongue came out, flicked like a snake's, and had gone.

We passed rows of commercial glasshouses on the left. My eyes strained to the right. I estimated two minutes and told Sarasini to stop and switch off. I got right out of the car to listen. There was the sound of the engine block cooling and a farm dog and a rustle of wind. No helicopter.

The line of pylons stretched from horizon to horizon. My eyes devoured the length and met no winking lights.

"They've gone to earth."

Sarasini got out and climbed on the roof of the car.

"There's a track just ahead that goes down to the right and into a bank of reeds, close by the nearest pylon. Beyond that a lot of water. It's too dark to see anything else."

I got out the map and checked with the little flashlight.

"It's a lake. Loosdrechtsche Plassen." My mouth was full of the Dutch syllables.

We got into the car and took the track down to the reeds on low beam. The reeds were in a strip a hundred metres wide and Sarasini killed the lights and took a final curve in the track with the engine cut out. The track ended at the edge of the water by three or four wooden cabins and a couple of boathouses. No helicopter, but that could be out of sight in a flattened patch of reeds and in one of the blank windows of a wooden cabin there could be the nose of a Schmeisser following the car. The BMW coasted to a halt.

We sat still.

Sound travels better over water because there are no natural obstacles to baffle it. We heard the woman's voice quite distinctly, thinned by distance. She spoke English and Sarasini turned to me.

"What did she say?"

"She said he was a fascist shit, that's why she killed him."

CHAPTER FIFTEEN

WITTEHUIS
FRIDAY 23 MARCH
3.15 A.M.

J udge an empire by what is stranded when the tide recedes.
The Romans left military roads and theatres. The British left law courts. The Americans left hulks rusting in the jungle. The Russians have never left. The Wehrmacht left concrete pillboxes.

The rain hung thin as a bridal veil across Loosdrechtsche Plassen, a white diffusion that hid the far side of the lake. The island lay in front of us, much closer now. There were three large bare trees with their toes almost in the water, and beside them a boathouse, and in a clearing with a commanding view of the lake was the concrete pillbox. The white house lay back eighty metres or so, its outline softened by tall shrubs, half a dozen windows showing subdued light.

We made cautious progress in *Zoet Meisje*. It was a five-metre dinghy from a boathouse on the shore and Sarasini had dismantled the mast to lower our profile. For the first couple of hundred metres he'd rowed standing up and facing forward like a Mediterranean fisherman. Now he shipped one oar because there is no way of rowing silently: an oar is a lever and the fulcrum is at the rowlock and if you want to make any progress then the transfer of energy at the fulcrum will produce friction and hence noise. Sarasini kneeled on the bottom boards and used one stubby oar as a paddle, trailing it in the water at the end of each stroke to correct our direction.

There was nothing we could do about the water dripping from the blade as he lifted the oar for the next stroke. The sound would carry a short way but the rustle of the wind in the dry reeds at the edge of the island would mask it.

We circled the island. It took thirty careful minutes. There was no sign of the helicopter but an area at the back of the house was shielded by conifers and lap-fencing and a garden shed, and there was space enough for a good pilot to put down.

"Well?" Sarasini dragged the oar in the water and we drifted to a halt.

We had seen nobody. This would be one of the lakes that people from Amsterdam and Utrecht and Hilversum used for boating and fishing, but in March there would only be week-enders. Our gang felt it wasn't worth a sentry. No, that was a false assumption: he could be in the pillbox sheltering from the rain or asleep.

I moved until I could mouth in Sarasini's ear. "We'll beach the boat. You guard it. I'll get into the house and collect the girl. Then we go back." I made it simple because there was no point in worrying about what I might meet until I reached the house.

"They got one of the pals … "

I felt his movement and put a hand on his shoulder. It was taut, the muscles bunched.

"I don't even want them to know we called."

"I can't go back and tell the *capo* his pal is sliced like salami and I did nothing about it. Willy was a good guy. He had guts."

His French was graphic: *Il avait des couilles au cul.* The whisper was hoarse and jerky.

We stayed immobile. The slatted wooden boards were sharp across my knees. I wanted to shake his shoulder. I wanted to scream abuse at him and at Fonza and his pals and at the ones who'd lifted the girl and at Crevecoeur who had got me on a lake in Holland in the middle of the night. Sarasini's stance was still very stiff.

"They have a load of Schmeissers and they're killers. Your *capo* is not here on this lake, alone, in the dark, with one little knife. Just forget the vendetta. This is what is going to happen: when we have the girl safe we are driving back to the last village and we're going to phone the Sûreté Nationale in Paris and the duty-officer can patch us through to Bonn or Château-Franqui or wherever Crevecoeur is. Forget Fonza's pals. Crevecoeur has his own pals in Dutch Security or the Green Berets and they can handle it. We are not going to war. These aren't bandits, these are fully armed terrorists."

His face was grey under the clouded night sky, drained of expression. His tongue came out to ease the pressure on his nerves. He shrugged my hand off and said, "*D'ac.*"

I thought he'd agreed.

We'd forgotten about the centreboard. It grated gently on stones as I jumped ashore by a wooden post with a smartly painted sign: *Wittehuis. Privaat. Verboden toegang.*

Perhaps the house had been a country retreat for a Nazi general and for thirty-five years the concrete pillbox had guarded it. I was the first invader. The problem was acute. It was squat and silent, with horizontal slits for eyes, and I couldn't tell in the dark whether somebody was watching my movements through rifle sights, choosing the right moment to squeeze the trigger.

I was under no illusions. We were not dealing with petty criminals or a conventional kidnap gang. Just one phrase carried across the water had defined the character of these people: "He was a fascist shit—that's why I killed him." They were politically motivated and if I posed any kind of threat I would be liquidated as a political undesirable. They believed in the bullet not the ballot.

I wanted to run, a crouching zigzag sprint from bush to bush, until I threw myself against the shelter of the concrete wall, out of sight of those slits in the pillbox. Instead I moved with desperate slowness because noise was the greatest threat: a wrong sound alerts the most bored sentry. My shoes had stayed in the dinghy and I felt every pebble pressing into the soles of my feet.

I went thirty metres. It took for ever.

I stood stock-still and checked the senses, not only eyes and ears but nose as well. In Vietnam it was the aroma of American tobacco that landed so many in ambushes. Nothing registered. I checked in through the low entrance and there was nothing inside.

And that was that. No danger. The pillbox and its concealed threat had been dominating the imagination and the relief I felt nearly killed me. It is during the release from tension that so many grow careless.

I checked back to the water and Sarasini was standing with the painter in his hand. I motioned for him to squat down and got a wave in return. There was no point in doing anything because even if I went back and stopped him standing as upright as a target on a rifle range there were a dozen other stupid ways he could behave. He was good in an alley, good behind the wheel of a car; he had no guile.

The German army had known the best position for a pillbox and it had contained nobody so now I moved towards the house with more confidence.

At fifty metres from the house I could make out that the shutters had not been closed but heavy drapes were drawn across the windows. The light showed through, dirty yellow.

At twenty metres I could distinguish there were also net curtains tied back in bunches, like every Dutch house.

At ten metres I saw the man with the sub-machine gun standing against the tree. The width of the trunk had masked him until his shoulders moved as he swung the gun barrel to target on my chest.

I froze.

It is remarkable how little the human body has adapted from the wild state. In a situation of mortal danger the responses are swift and totally automatic. Adrenalin passes into the blood-stream to prepare for imminent explosive action. Breathing rate and pulse increase to feed in extra oxygen. Blood leaves the stomach to swell the muscles. The eyes widen to admit maximum information. Even the hairs rise though on humans this no longer presents an intimidating spectacle.

At the training place in Virginia they demonstrate all this with both videotape and live examples. Every one of my intake had to be a live example and sensors recorded pulse, breathing, sweat, all the indicators of fear. Each trainee was put into a danger situation tailored to an individual phobia: I had had a Black Widow spider placed on my naked belly.

I heard the metallic click.

The reason the human species advanced out of the jungle is not because of physical responses but mental activity. Major Surtee, our F2 Instructor, said the human body was adapted to deal with an encounter-situation in a swamp with a plesiosaurus; but it took the human brain to triumph in an encounter-situation with another human. He'd said: "Survivors are the ones whose brains work. It's called natural selection."

I had registered the snap and my subconscious interpreted safety-catch released and now my brain had considered the possibilities for action and selected the least fatal and I said:

"Don't. You'll only alert my friends."

My voice was low. It was for his ears only. Also I wanted to draw him nearer to me. We were too close to the house and I didn't want to bring any more of them out through the front door. This one might genuinely have missed our quiet arrival in the dinghy or have just returned from peeing in the bushes or might have a set route to patrol.

Silence. He didn't believe me. Or he didn't understand English. I spoke only tourist Dutch and there was no point in trying *Waar is bet Amerikaanse Consulaat?*

I tried French because they'd done the kidnapping in Paris: *"Ne tirez pas. J'ai des…"*

"Stuff it."

He closed the distance between us, wary as a scorpion.

"Raise your hands."

Good. I'd need the hands raised.

His accent was that mid-Atlantic intonation they teach in schools in Germany and Sweden.

I saw it clearly, the 9 mm Walther SMG, recognizable because of its metal stock. Distinctive. The stock folds forward for close-quarter firing. It was folded forward now and he kept his index finger curled round the trigger and patted over my body with his left hand.

No sounds came from the house. There was a light breeze from the west, fitful, and it made a sigh through a clump of dry reeds like silk material rustling across skin.

"Who are you?" he asked.

I'd had the opportunity to reassess. I regretted my first words but at the time they'd seemed necessary to delay his shooting. Now I could no longer pretend I had stumbled ashore on the island by mistake or for fun. The danger I was in was absolute and immediate because the gun barrel levelled at the lower part of my chest and if I moved by one centimetre his trigger finger would close, in the fraction of a second it took the impulse to travel from his brain.

He shuffled a half pace away from me, the SMG raising slightly, tensed because of my silence. He was very close to firing. I replied: "You wouldn't know our group."

It was the best I could do: deflect his interest away from me to others who might be concealed in the shrubs.

"What are you? How many of you?" His voice had risen slightly and that was right because it indicated the onset of uncertainty.

The line I walked on was so thin it was non-existent. I said: "The Ultras." If he panicked he would squeeze the trigger. If he needed help he would shout. All I could do was increase his uncertainty because a brain that is busy coping with meaningless information is a fraction slower to react.

"Ultras?"

I was registering his features now, just the dark wells of his eyes, the curves of a moustache, hair to the shoulders.

"What the shit are you talking about?"

I had to make him move the barrel. The lungs extend as far down as the second rib and he was aimed to puncture my lungs.

"You're too late," I said. "We've come for the helicopter."

Now.

His reaction was instantaneous. He jerked his head forty-five degrees because over there was where the helicopter was hidden. His torso moved with his head, the SMG pointing to the extremity of my rib-cage, and I took a half-step sideways with my hand already swinging down to chop the tendons in his wrist when the knife hit him in the throat.

The noise it made going in was soft and sexual.

He died gasping for breath, his windpipe severed, his finger locked tight round the trigger, down on his knees, the barrel waving blindly in an arc in front of him, explosive gases flashing in the dark, percussion stabbing my eardrums, sinking to one elbow, then convulsing on the ground.

I'd thrown myself prone when the night erupted and after the sub-machine gun's violence ceased I could hear a couple of dozen paces behind me high-pitched screams from Sarasini where the wild shooting had scythed through him.

I was on my feet and making for Sarasini with some notion of dragging him back to the boat when lights on the exterior wall of the house and the landing stage and the boathouse caught me. A door behind me was flung open.

"Stop. Stop. Stop."

I turned edge on to the newcomer because that way the target presented is only half as broad as the full width of your back. There were two men in the doorway of the house. One stepped forward and knelt on the ground by the man with the knife in his throat.

"Fucking killed Franz."

He got to his feet and walked towards me with a pistol in his hand and he was raising it as he got close when Sarasini started to scream again. The man with the pistol veered aside and took quick steps to where Sarasini lay clutching his belly.

Without any pause the man put the pistol to Sarasini's temple and shot him.

The screaming came to a dead stop.

In the sudden silence I heard the wind in the reeds and the sound of a child crying from the house.

CHAPTER SIXTEEN

"Fucking bourgeois spy. Kill her. Kill her now. Fucking pig-woman."

For a moment she had the look of a horse in panic, white showing all round her eyes, mane of dark hair astray, tendons stark in her neck, head skewed. She was trying to get at me, desperate to lay her hands on me.

"I'm going to kill her. Why don't you kill her? You're not a man. I'm going to strangle the shit. Take your hands off me."

"Cool it."

"They murdered Franz. Let me alone. That American fucker is going to die."

"Okay, Ulrike, not yet."

They spoke English. Franz, the dead one, had a German name. Ulrike, with the wild hatred in her eyes, must also be German. But they spoke English.

"Now. She shouldn't breathe another second. She's a fascist pig-woman. Leave go of me. Tell him to leave off, Yussif."

The one who held her back had long blond hair and a blond beard. The other man stood against the wall under the light. He wore slightly tinted glasses. His shirt was unbuttoned to reveal a medallion on a chain against a background of black matted hair. His skin was dark and with Yussif for a name he'd come from one of the Arab countries. He had the eyes of a poker player, a face as impassive as the jack of spades. He flicked the fingers of a hand at her and kept his silence. The other hand held a pistol, pointing loosely at my feet.

Every detail was acid-etched on my brain because my death was in the air, so close I could feel the coldness.

"I'm going to tear the heart out of her."

The woman had no weapon. She wanted to get her hands on me. She jerked her body from side to side, and then the passion drained away. She stopped the struggle and stood breathing in great waves.

"Okay, Vratko, let go of me. I'm easy now." The voice was calm.

The blond-haired man, Vratko, held her arm twisted high up behind her back and either she had no combat-training or was too blinded with hate to counter the armlock. He let her go now and she stood a moment rubbing at the grip-marks on her wrist, her eyes flickering over me.

"Right," Ulrike said, "inside."

Ulrike's eyes were sunk in bowls of shadow cast by the wall light but there was venom showing in the tilt of her chin towards me.

"And Franz and the other?" asked Vratko.

"Later," she said. "We can bury all three together."

There was authority in the way she spoke, even if the others had been restraining her.

She went through the front door first and Yussif had the gun on my back as I followed in.

It was called the White House but not from any resemblance to 1600 Pennsylvania Avenue. The builders had carved 1932 in the white stucco above the lintel and the large square entrance hall was cluttered with ageing furniture of the period, the lumpy stuff not Mies van der Rohe. There was a settee with faded floral cushions, two fat armchairs, a stuffed fish in a glass case, and next to an umbrella stand was a big wooden chest and on top a green glass bowl with a neat pile of hand grenades, as if it were an arrangement of oranges. The man Vratko pushed past and gathered up the bowl in case it gave me ideas.

I heard the sound of crying from upstairs again.

"Cathy," Ulrike shouted. "The bloody child's crying."

The door to my left jerked open and a girl stood for a moment inspecting our faces, very serious. She looked no more than eighteen. She had mouse-coloured hair gathered in an elastic band and wore faded jeans and a Berkeley sweatshirt. She held a submachine gun.

She said: "I was covering you from the window."

Ulrike said: "Go and shut the child up."

Cathy nodded, her tail of hair bouncing, her pale eyes devoid of expression. There was no blemish on her cheeks, no lines on her forehead, she was a flawless doll. She sauntered up to me and prodded the machine pistol under my left breast.

"Bang, bang," Cathy said. "You're dead."

She'd been eating an apple. The sweetness of it was on her breath. She climbed up the stairs, humming a repetitive little phrase. It was "Yellow Submarine".

Nobody would live permanently on an island in the middle of this lake and I decided the place must be a holiday home, possibly broken into. The lumpy furniture would be the cast-off stuff from the town house and in the living room would be the sort of furniture you get in a place that is used only in summer and at week-ends: cane chairs, a rug with a worn patch, occasional tables that nested into each other, Cézanne prints behind glass.

But it had been entirely furnished by a rich man. I was prodded by the gun into a room with black leather and chrome chairs, a white sofa, smoked glass tables, a shaggy pile carpet over a polished wood-block floor, quadrophonic speakers and a slimline amplifier and playing deck. In one corner a plant with huge glossy leaves clambered to the ceiling.

Ulrike was lighting a cigarette. The flame trembled slightly, the hands showing the aftermath of her hysteria.

"Who are you?"

"My name's Cody."

"That means nothing to me. Who are you? Who do you work for?"

"I don't work for anybody."

"Then why are you here?"

I must have glanced aside at the heavy drapes drawn across the window because she said: "Don't even think of it. Yussif will shoot you. We're not going to kill you yet, so Yussif will aim for a foot or a knee. He is expert with the gun. It was his training."

I studied Yussif leaning against the wall. He seemed to like the reassurance of a wall at his back. There was no movement in him at all while I looked: there is a calmness about those who wait, finger on trigger, for a man to walk into the cross-hairs.

"Who was the other one?" she asked.

"A fool who believed he could play tricks with knives."

"He killed Franz. He murdered our comrade and that is why we will kill you."

She might have been ordering a kilo of potatoes, her voice was so matter-of-fact. I had little doubt: these were the people who'd arranged for Desnos to be murdered. Vratko had finished off Sarasini and Yussif held a gun on me now, but I felt it would be Ulrike who'd given the word to have my friend killed.

"That's what you believe in, isn't it? Killing people, I mean."

The blond Vratko stirred: I wasn't supposed to use that tone with them. It wasn't bravado on my part. I had to find out about these people, I had to prod under the stone to see what crawled out.

She said: "We believe in eliminating fascist elements in our society."

I felt the chill in me. They all like to clothe their purpose in phrases but whether they call it *eliminating fascist elements* or *pacification* or *the final solution* it means the same.

"I call it killing people."

The smoke from her cigarette drifted into her eyes, sting-ing, and she shook her head. "There are fascist elements in capitalist society, greedy, corrupt, exploiting, dangerous. They are no better than boils and you must take a surgical knife to them and let out the poison. There is no other way to cleanse your society. If you insist on the expression: yes, kill them. They have had their chance and they do not reform. They continue to commit crimes for which they are condemned. We carry out the executions."

"You dislike their politics. You cannot persuade enough people to agree with you and so you kill."

"Who was the first to kill tonight?" Vratko said. "Your friend with the knife killed Franz."

Ulrike paid him no attention. She stared at me, devoured me with dark eyes.

"Do you dislike the politics of Hitler?" she asked.

"Hitler has nothing to do with the people you want to kill."

"Hitler was evil and if he'd been liquidated the world would have been a better place. Can you deny that?"

There are no answers when someone resurrects Hitler to jus-tify their actions.

Ulrike continued: "If Hitler had been assassinated, you would have applauded the person who did it. Instead your so-called democracies continued to deal with Hitler, encouraged him, right until the moment of war. The virus of his politics lives on in Western imperialist states and we are eliminating it. You should give us medals instead of denouncing us."

I asked: "Who are you?" I knew the nature of the people, but they'd have a name. They always do. A name bestows importance.

She replied: "We are Blood Group O."

"The dawn is red? Blood is red?" I remembered the slogans daubed on Amsterdam walls and the man who'd weighed me up before spraying on the initials BGO.

"Our time has come," she said. "Blood Group O is the third generation from Germany. Each year we grow, our links with comrades in the struggle in other countries become stronger. When the imperialists cut one of us down, three more grow in his place. We have arms, we have money, we have safe houses, we have co-operation with liberation movements everywhere."

"With the PLO and so on," I said.

She made a noise as if she were spitting out a strand of tobacco. Her eyes never wavered from my face. "They are middle-aged, they have become reactionary. You know what Lenin said?"

"Many things."

"He said that on their thirtieth birthday revolutionaries should be taken out and shot because they have lost their zeal."

"The PFLP then."

"Everywhere in the capitalist countries we have brave comrades," she said. "The Red Army in Japan. Here in Holland, Rode Hulp. In Italy, the Red Brigades. In Uruguay, the Tupamaros. In Ireland, the IRA."

"Brave comrades," I agreed, watching her face. A lock of hair had fallen to mask one eye. "It must take guts to shoot someone in the back."

She ignored the taunt and in her solidity I sensed a considerable person. I had seen one side of her when the blood-lust had come out and had its brief run. It would be unusual for her to display the rawness of her feelings and to that extent I was privileged. She was the leader, acknowledged or not. The others watched and waited on her, and if they'd restrained her from clawing at me it was because I had some value to them.

She said: "There is little point in talking with you because your mind is closed. You have been brainwashed by the capitalist press. Your own bourgeois prejudices blind you to the possibility of any better society. You must understand that is why we kill you, why we kill the political and business leaders of your reactionary regimes, why we kill your so-called innocents. Nobody in your society is innocent who allows it to continue exploiting the masses, the Third World, blacks and women."

"You're talking to a woman."

I needn't have reminded her. She dragged smoke into her lungs while she inspected my body and then stabbed out her cigarette. "Having tits doesn't make you a woman. You're nothing more than the agent of reactionary powers."

"Nobody tells me what to do."

"You misunderstand. You live in a rich and oppressive society. You choose to live in it. Therefore you condone it."

I looked round the expensively furnished room. "Is this your house? I don't admire your hypocrisy. What you've spent in this one room would feed an entire village in India for a year."

"And I don't admire your cynicism. We have sympathizers now in all levels of society. We have rich people who support us because they see their previous life was immoral."

"Like Poelsma."

She was five paces across the room and I thought the bloodlust was up in her again as she reached for my sweater and bunched it in her fist.

"Who told you about Poelsma? Who are you? Who do you work for? Why have you come?"

Her face was close to mine. I stared into her eyes, a long way into her eyes. It was like staring into a tunnel and seeing dark at the end.

I could have taken her in that moment while her body shielded me from Yussif's gun, and the moment passed while I stared.

"Sssst."

It was Yussif who hissed but I'd caught it too, faint first then louder, the sound of a boat's outboard motor.

Ulrike lifted a corner of the curtain and peered out. Dawn would come soon but at the moment it was crow-black.

The throttle cut back quite close to the island, and died. It was silent outside, and in the living room, and in the whole house. The child no longer wept.

Vratko stood in the doorway again. I had been so absorbed in Ulrike I hadn't noticed his exit. He nodded at her.

Vratko stood aside and another man came throught the door and stopped. It was as if he'd blundered by mistake on stage in the middle of the second act and none of the actors quite knew what to do about it.

Yussif gestured with his gun hand. "Don't walk in front of her." It was the first time I'd heard him speak. His voice was guttural, reminding me of someone else. I was too tired to think who.

The newcomer stared at me. He was older than the others. There was a puffiness about his eyes as if he had a sleep debt like me.

"Who is she?" he asked.

Ulrike said: "We're just coming on to that. Have you heard about … ?"

"Yes."

"He has it set up?"

"Yes."

"No hitches?"

"No." He was irritated by the questioning and abruptly turned the focus on me. "How did she get here?"

Well, she didn't swim," Ulrike said. "There will be a boat pushed into the reeds. She came with a man and they've killed Franz."

"Killed Franz?" It was too much to take in at the end of the night. He knuckled an eye and shook his head and looked at me. "You … ?"

"No, the man she came with used a knife."

"Christ."

"At least the pig is dead too. He was hit in the stomach by Franz's Schmeisser and Vratko finished him off with a bullet in the brain."

He lost focus on me, the look in his eyes receding inwards in shock. He lacked their ruthless determination. This one wasn't a fanatical member of Blood Group O and possibly it was something I could work on.

"Is this your house?" I asked.

The two of them spoke together. He said, "Yes," and Ulrike said, "It's not your business."

"What's your name?"

"Van Berkel."

"Don't answer her questions." Dark anger suffused Ulrike's face. "She's no right to be asking questions." And to me: "We ask the questions, you answer. Why did you come to Wittehuis?"

"To get the girl back, Poelsma's little girl."

"Poelsma's screwing us," she screamed. "The double-crossing rich pig. I'm going to slice that girl's ears off and send them to him for screwing us."

"What's eating you? Cut out the hysterics. Poelsma's doing okay. I told you it was all set up." Van Berkel turned to me. "Does Poelsma know you're here?"

The temptation was there to suggest Poelsma was betraying them and I hesitated. All of them were living close to the edge of their nerves and if I gave a nudge I thought they would be over and fighting among themselves. But Ulrike mad would be a danger both to me and Poelsma's little girl.

"No."

"How did you find out?" van Berkel went on.

"The girl's nanny."

"Did she contact you?"

"Don't be stupid," Ulrike said. "Nannies don't do things like that. She's lying."

"You've got to restrain yourself." Van Berkel contained his irritation; none showed in his face, but he had his hands clasped behind his back and the fingers were lacing together. "If you want to discover anything from this woman, you must let her speak. She has been able to uncover this base, where the child is being held, and we need to know what else she knows. Now," he turned back to me, "are you a friend of the Poelsmas or the nanny?"

"I'll tell you what it is." I'd had a little time to think. "I do a certain sort of work, call it private investigations, and in the course of that I have naturally made contacts in the Paris underworld."

"Keep quiet." Ulrike had been about to speak and van Berkel rounded on her. We waited in spiky silence and then van Berkel turned back to me. "Continue."

"Poelsma's nanny was very upset about the kidnapping and angry that Poelsma wouldn't go to the police and she asked a lawyer friend to recommend someone who could trace the girl unofficially. He was a criminal lawyer with one or two gang members among his clients. Anyway the outcome was I was hired and came to Holland with Sarasini, who was supposed to have contacts in Amsterdam. He heard a whisper the girl was on this island."

"How?"

"I never asked his sources and now you've killed him you can't find out. That's how I'm here."

"What was the name of this lawyer?"

"Poussignac."

He made me spell it.

"He was a *notaire*?"

"I suppose so."

Van Berkel gave a pale smile. He nodded and I decided my story had been filed away in a retentive brain for later analysis.

"And what were you going to do?"

"Push open a window, locate the girl, take her back to Paris."

"And now you've been caught…"

He waved a hand instead of finishing the sentence. Nobody mentioned the possibility of paying ransom money because that wasn't what Blood Group O wanted. Poelsma was away organizing that.

We heard her coming down the stairs and she was singing softly as she opened the door. " '…Yellow Submarine, Yellow Submarine, We all live in…' Hi Piet." Cathy stood in the doorway, fist clenched in salute to van Berkel, a grin breaking the smoothness of her face. "It's okay, Ulrike, I told her a story and she's sleeping again. She's kind of cute. Seems a shame, know what I mean?"

Her accent was West Coast, California, land of the freaks, breeding ground of Charles Manson's family. It's where all the weirdos stop because if they go any further they fall off the edge of America.

CHAPTER SEVENTEEN

"What was his name?"

I had to think hard what I'd told them. "Poussignac."

"There's no notary of that name listed in the Paris volume of Bottin." Van Berkel pushed a hand through his dark curls. Over the ears there were touches of grey that could have come out of a bottle.

"Maybe it was an assumed name. Maybe he didn't practise in Paris."

"If he had Paris clients, he'd be listed in Paris. Did you meet Poussignac?"

"Yes." I could see the danger. He'd already been on the phone to somebody to look through Bottin, and now he was back at me. He was cautious or suspicious and needed convincing with detail. Because if I didn't convince him, one of the others would take over. And if I ruffled Ulrike's authority, I'd suffer her mad streak.

"In his office?"

"Yes."

"Then you must have seen his name on the office door, or looked for a plate at the entrance to the building."

"Perhaps if it had been daylight. But in the dark it wasn't possible."

"In that case," he looked directly at me, "how did you know it was his office?"

"He sat behind the desk."

"No, I mean how did you know you'd come to the right address?"

"I was taken."

"And you made an assumption?"

"I made a deduction, perhaps it was invalid, but I had no reason to think so. I was telephoned by an acquaintance who said he'd heard of a possible job ... "

"Just a minute. What was the name of this acquaintance?"

I could muddy the water about Poussignac, suggesting he might have used a false name. I could hardly try a similar trick with a person I knew. I couldn't give a false name. Neither could I bring in Fonza, for instance. They'd have a way of checking. They had, after all, some connection with the Marsiale gang who'd gunned down my friend Desnos.

I paused until he began to frown. "Be your age." I spoke with tired resignation. "You know better than to ask a question like that. I can't have you knocking on the doors of everyone I know in Paris."

Yussif stirred where he stood against the wall by the climbing plant. Van Berkel had insisted he question me without the presence of the others because of the tensions and interruptions, and Ulrike had made another furious outburst. Van Berkel had just shrugged and said: "You see how hopeless it is? We haven't time for these dramas." Only Yussif had stayed because they wanted a gun kept on me.

Van Berkel said: "We'll return to that. Carry on."

"I was rung up and told a lawyer called Poussignac had a job for me. I was picked up at eight o'clock on Wednesday evening and driven to the car park under place du Parvis and we went on foot to Ile Saint-Louis. The office was upstairs in one of those big old houses in rue Saint-Louis. There was a man in a dark business suit waiting, sitting behind a desk, reading some papers out of a file. I made the deduction: Poussignac. There you are."

Van Berkel noticed somebody had been playing a record and left the player on. He walked over and the little light blinked off.

I said: "Anyway … " I left it hanging in the air. I didn't like the interrogation, but the thing about interrogations is that you can make them yield information in the reverse direction. I would make van Berkel tell me things I didn't know. I waited until he turned his attention back to me.

"Anyway what?"

"What difference does it make who he was? He gave me the job."

"Of course it matters," he said, irritated. "Supposing it wasn't Poussignac the lawyer. Then who would it be? Poussignac the criminal? Poussignac the policeman? Poussignac the spy?" He relaxed, smiling at me, seeing if I would choose an alternative.

"Yes, he could be one of those." I was indifferent. "If you find out he wasn't a lawyer, I'll consider that."

"We'll check if Poussignac the lawyer exists. Don't worry, we'll check. Who was at this meeting?"

"Poussignac, myself, the knife-artist Sarasini who is dead, and Miss Tulloch. Nobody else. The rest of the offices were dark."

"Miss Tulloch … ?"

"Simone's nanny."

"Of course. I didn't know she had a name. Describe her."

"She had grey hair, a Scottish accent, believes in God and self-discipline."

"Yes," he said. "What did she say?"

I repeated most of the story of the kidnapping. Van Berkel nodded once or twice.

"So you agreed to trace Simone?"

"Yes."

"Even though you knew that Poelsma had left Paris also to try and get Simone back?"

"I knew that Simone was being held under duress, that the police hadn't been called in, and if *I* rescued Simone then that would guarantee no harm would come to her."

"How much?"

"What do you mean?"

"Poelsma has not been consulted about hiring you. The nanny will not be rich. How much are you being paid?"

"Nothing."

He had thick eyebrows to match his headful of curls and he raised them. I was a mercenary and they don't depress the market by being altruistic.

"I owed somebody a favour. Now I don't."

Van Berkel considered this and then went to the window. He peered between the drapes at the first thin morning light.

"I think it's going to be a fine day. Though in Holland you can never give a weather forecast for more than thirty minutes ahead." He sighed and continued in the same conversational tone: *"Die Liebe ist kälter als der Tod, nicht war?"* He turned his head from the window, smiling, to encourage an answer.

"I don't speak Dutch," I replied.

"German." He was searching my face for the betraying little signs of surprise and anxiety. "We only have your word for it that you are British and living in Paris. Perhaps you are French, working for the Sûreté, and Poelsma did run to them for help. Perhaps you are German, working for their secret police. Franz was German, you see, and Ulrike. Though not Yussif, Vratko, Cathy and Mogens."

"I haven't met Mogens."

"Danish. A regular little United Nations."

"Blood Group O."

"Yes. They take their name from the martyrs of Stammheim Prison. I find it a little melodramatic, but I suppose it is necessary."

"Necessary?" Distaste and disbelief mingled in my voice. He glanced at me and wandered round the room, touching his possessions, reassuring himself of their presence.

"Like your so-called Poussignac, I too am a lawyer, but an advocate. Much of my work involves cases at the High Court in Amsterdam. Like doctors and police, lawyers see only a sick side of society. Or to be more precise, we see those people our society has corrupted or disapproves of. Franz was a client of mine, the man you killed."

"It wasn't me."

"You were an accessory. Oh don't worry, we've had no death penalty in Holland for over a century."

"You have Yussif."

Van Berkel brushed at something in front of his face. Then he clasped his hands behind his back, teetered on his toes and gave me a courtroom lecture.

"Franz was very much disapproved of by bourgeois society, rejected is not too strong a word, bullied and hunted by authority as if he were a mad dog. It started as far back as 1972, and Franz has been on the run ever since. Well, he doesn't have to run any more. Some of the time he lived in hiding in Germany but mostly it was in Amsterdam, on occasions openly, for the last few months in hiding since the Germans have been putting pressure on the ministry to cancel his residence permit. They wanted him back where they could watch him, you see, monitor his contacts, check his mail, bug his telephone, trip him up with petty offences, put him behind bars again, perhaps arrange an accident."

"And he'd done nothing criminal?"

"How many people have criminal pasts in West Germany? By criminal, I mean those who have gone to jail. Fifty thousand? Sixty thousand? Are they persecuted after they come out or are they given a chance to rehabilitate? And that's leaving aside the war criminals still unpunished from the Nazi regime—the State lets hundreds of thousands of them live in peace. No, it was the nature of Franz's offence the German Federal State could not tolerate: it was political."

Like a policeman, a lawyer always wants to question. But after the cross-examination comes the speech for the defence. I asked: "What precisely had he done?"

"In June 1972 the leaders of the Red Army Faction were arrested: Baader, Ennslin, Raspe, so on. They were accused of murdering four US soldiers stationed in Federal Germany and the authorities linked Franz's name with them because they wanted to discredit him. His terrible crime had been to be one of the organizers of the Socialist Patients' Collective while he was a student at Heidelberg University. He went into hiding under an assumed name in Amsterdam and when he was discovered I was appointed his lawyer to fight his case. We lost. Franz was deported to West Germany where there were no terrorist crimes they could charge him with. Instead they imprisoned him for being a member of the Collective which they had conveniently outlawed as a 'criminal association' under article 129 of their criminal code. This Patients' Collective had been started by marxist intellectuals who practised anti-psychiatry; they maintained that conventional psychiatrists were an arm of the capitalist State, a concealed form of institutional violence to control those whose illness had actually been caused by capitalism."

I couldn't tell whether he believed in this himself or whether he was merely repeating Franz's theory. I suggested: "It was the Western counterpart to the Institutes for the Criminally Insane they have in the Soviet Union?"

"What would you know? That's just propaganda. Have you ever been in one?"

The one I'd escaped from in East Germany—where they'd shown me the rabid dog that would bite me if I weren't satisfactory in my answers. I didn't tell him.

"What precisely was criminal about this Patients' Collective?" I asked. "There are a lot of people with way-out ideas who aren't banned."

"Soon there will be no freedom left in West Germany. It is going the same way as the Nazi Reich, with State power choking freedom to death."

"But what had they done?"

"The story was that a raid had turned up some guns and explosives but the police would have planted that as evidence."

"You mean like the Browning Automatic?" I pointed at Yussif. "And the helicopter and the sub-machine guns and the bowl of hand grenades. Are they planted?" There was a pause and I thought it was worth a try. "Why are they necessary?"

Van Berkel turned again to the window. He drew the curtains fully back. "This room faces east. It's really marvellous watching the sun rise over the lake."

CHAPTER EIGHTEEN

WITTEHUIS
FRIDAY 23 MARCH
8.20 A.M.

"I have telephoned Paris."

In normal circumstances I wake without altering my breathing pattern, quickly and cleanly. It was part of the Virginia training. But after a couple of hours' sleep I was still a dozen on the negative side and van Berkel's voice drifted into my brain, tangling with the dream that was so vivid. We know a lot about the human body but we don't understand dreams.

"I spoke to someone in the judicial Syndicat there and the point is this."

I once heard a theory that dreaming was the mind slipping the constraints of time and visiting the future; Freud of course made sexual interpretations, and from our own experience we know we can solve problems while we dream. They've gone and carried out experiments that prove dreams are essential and deprived of dreams a human becomes mentally disturbed.

Yet still we do not understand dreams.

Why should I dream of Sarasini's tongue? Freud would have had something to say.

"Their records show only one notary called Poussignac and he currently practises at Cahors, several hundred kilometres from Paris. Your story appears to be false."

My brain was clearing, the dream no longer dominant. It had been of the moment of Sarasini's death, a slow-motion replay of the night's events. I had dreamed in black and white and shades of grey except for the blood, and the blood flowed red from his mouth. In my dream Sarasini had bitten clean through his tongue and Freud would have had something to say about that too.

"Now, is it because you are lying or because you have been tricked?"

Van Berkel was in his cross-examination stance, legs apart, hands behind his back. He looked down at me on the bed. My wrists had been tied with thin cord and linked to the brass head-rail of the bed. My ankles were bound to the footrail. Vratko had done it, drawing the cord too tight, constricting the bloodflow and now my hands were numbed and cold.

"You maintain your name is Cody and you are British. As in everything we have only your word. You have no papers."

"They're in my bag."

"And where is that?"

"The hotel in Amsterdam. I left my bag in Sarasini's room."

"Were you lovers?"

"Oh for God's sake."

I pushed the memory of the dream out of my mind.

"What do you know of these people?"

His question wrong-footed me and I queried: "You mean Sarasini?"

"No. What do you know of Blood Group O?"

He used the name with a certain reluctance because it forced him to acknowledge their purpose.

"They're cold-blooded and inflexible. They kidnapped a little girl and threatened to cut off her ears. They blackmailed the father. They kill and aren't particular who they kill. They murder quite casually. I think they take pleasure in it. There has always been a tiny minority of human beings who have a taste for blood, enjoying the power of killing. These have simply invented a convenient ideology. Ulrike, who seems so clever and articulate—really she wanted nothing better than to attack me with her hands. Cathy is unthinking, a child pulling off the wings of an insect. But Ulrike is something else: violent, bigoted, contemptuous of others."

"Stop it. You don't know her. She's … "

He cut himself off because he was betraying personal feelings and an interrogator should never do that.

"You found this place," he said. "How?"

He was retracing his previous questions, trying to trip. "Sarasini had heard about this lake and we saw the helicopter come down. Is it yours too?"

"It's hired, borrowed, stolen. It's not important. What have you found out about the plan?"

"Only this. Poelsma knew Ulrike and the others already. Another rich bourgeois sympathizer like you, I guess. But even so he had to be blackmailed into doing something for them. Therefore it is something that is very dangerous to Poelsma. Physically dangerous or else the danger that his connection with terrorists will be exposed."

"Guerrillas," he said.

His hands caught my attention. They were clasped behind his back, the fingers flexing and twining together like lovers. He was nervous and an advocate, used to courtroom cross-examinations, shouldn't be nervous. He asked his questions and I gave my answers and he sifted through the fragments trying to grasp the implications for him and Blood Group O. The fingers twisted because it was urgent. The operation was running. It was a matter of a day or two, of hours even.

He changed tack. "Describe this lawyer Poussignac. How did he speak? Did he speak French to you?"

"Yes."

"What sort of accent?"

"I'm British. You don't expect … "

"The Parisians elide their syllables, their lips scarcely seem to move. Was he like that?"

I shrugged. I was tired of this fictional character I had brought in. I had invented him as a hinge between Poelsma's nanny and myself. If van Berkel himself hadn't been a lawyer, he would never have taken such an interest in him.

"What was his face like? How old was he?"

"About fifty or fifty-five years old. Dark straight hair, greying a little, a bristly moustache, solidly built but not fat, glasses with black frames. He was short, a little more than my height."

"Like a million other Frenchmen. Did he wear a red flash in his lapel? A man of his age might have done resistance work against the Nazis."

"No."

"Like a million other Frenchmen." He paced to the window and returned. "Sarasini. He wasn't your lover, you say. Was he a friend?"

"No. He was in the ... " I stopped. But you can't call the words back, not even when they've betrayed you.

His eyes caught mine and I tried to appear casual.

"Finish what you were going to say. He wasn't a friend; he was ... ?"

"In Poussignac's room when I arrived."

"So." He made his half dozen paces to the window and returned. "Somebody you knew in the criminal underworld in Paris gave your name to this lawyer. When you arrive for the meeting, the gangster Sarasini is there—for I assume an expert with a knife has a criminal background. He accompanies you to Amsterdam because he has connections, presumably criminal, in that city. Yes, yes." He ran his hand through his curls. "Now we're making progress. I was careless not to have pursued your criminal connections before. It is Ulrike who knows the right people to telephone in Paris."

He smiled at me before he left.

And I lay on the bed, knowing how stupid I'd been. I'd done it because my brain was tired, but that was no excuse. I'd said I'd had contacts in the underworld and so of course did they. They had used four men from the Marsiale gang to shoot down Desnos. Ulrike would phone her Parisian contacts and enquire about me. No, they would tell Ulrike, this woman Cody is no pal of ours, she must have links with Fonza's family; and the whisper would come that I had been Desnos's friend, his *petite amie* even, and we all know about Desnos: Desnos worked for the Sûreté.

After shouting for a minute or so I heard Yellow Submarine climbing the stairs.

"What is it?" she asked.

"I'd like some coffee."

"Please," she corrected.

"Please." For God's sake.

She didn't look tired from the lack of sleep. When you're eighteen you can take anything and come up smiling.

Cathy was gone fifteen minutes and minutes could be important. I had no illusions whatever about them. They had killed Desnos and Willy de Groot and Sarasini. I was kept alive because I was an unknown danger and once they had found out about me there would be no further reason to keep me alive.

Her doll-face was absolutely composed when she returned with the cup of coffee. "I had to wait for it to pass through a filter paper into a jug," she said. "There was no instant in the kitchen. Hey, you know what they say down in Mexico? *Nescafé, no es café.* Neat, right? I was down in Mex with my boyfriend before this came up."

I said: "I can't drink it with my wrists tied."

She considered this and smiled. The smile made the smallest of dimples in her cheeks.

"No way," she said. "I'll feed it into you."

I raised my head off the pillow and she sat next to me on the bed, holding the cup to my lips.

"Like feeding a sick kid," Cathy said.

"Young Simone," I suggested.

"She's too grown up to be fed. She can manage on her own."

"She's not trussed up like a chicken."

"Nope. We locked her door. Should hold her."

"Sure," I agreed. "She's only a little kid. She's not too hot with a machine gun yet."

"Listen, do you want this coffee or not, feller?" Her voice was taut, a little cross. I'd never seen anyone get cross without showing anything in the face.

"Thanks for the coffee," I said. "I'm glad it was you came up the stairs. I was scared if it was Ulrike she wouldn't make me any coffee."

"Ulrike's fine. Don't you badmouth her."

"All I meant was she doesn't approve of me."

"No, you're the class enemy. She says we must never yield to the class enemy, we must be ruthless, we must have nothing to do with them, even if they're our family. We must cut them off like a rotten branch from a tree."

It was like a schoolgirl crush on a teacher, shining in her face.

"She really is something, know what I mean? A couple of years back she called round at this friend of her father, some rich industrialist pig, and he asked her in of course. So when she was in his study she pulled a gun and took money from his safe and then shot him in the legs so he couldn't run after her. She's strong, Ulrike, she's got balls."

She lifted the cup to my lips again.

"I put two sugars in," Cathy said. "I hope that's not too sweet."

"No, it's fine." Sugar was twenty calories per spoon, pure energy. The odds were a hundred to one I wouldn't turn Cathy and then I'd need the energy. I drank some more. "What were you doing down in Mexico? Holiday?"

"Sort of. Craig had these friends he wanted to visit with in Mexico City and I went along for the ride. Then we had a bust-up, you know how it is, I was a little soft on one of the other guys. Mogens, matter of fact."

"Mogens. I haven't met him yet."

"He's still sleeping. He just crashed out when he flew back last night. Mogens is really into sleeping, know what I mean? He looks cute when he sleeps. Defenceless."

"Most people look like that when they sleep. It's the muscles in the face relaxing. They no longer defend the face against the world."

"Is that a fact?" Her eyes were wide and round. "You're kind of smart, aren't you? Like Ulrike. I never had a college education."

"Me neither."

"My folks wanted me to go to college. My pa is a big-shot executive at Boeing and they thought it was right I should go to college. But I'm not into books."

"What do you need the helicopter for?" I asked.

"To get away, of course."

"Get away?"

"Sure, you know, after."

"After what?"

She clammed again, putting the cup to my lips.

"A helicopter has a pretty limited range," I said. "Mogens can't fly you far. You won't be safe if you're doing something, well, big."

"Gosh, it's big right enough. But Mogens will fly us to Copenhagen and we'll pick up a jet there. He was trained as a pilot in the Danish Air Force. We'll make it somewhere friendly. Algeria, Libya. Yussif will fix it."

"You think the Danes will just hand over a jet plane?"

"Well, we've got the Schmeissers and some explosives and we've got the girl."

"I see."

"Don't you want any more coffee?"

"In a minute."

"It's really tingly. Like the feeling I had as a kid, waiting for Christmas. I'm really into revolution, know what I mean?"

"Killing people."

"You shut up. I don't go for that kind of talk." Cathy brushed back a strand of hair that had escaped from the elastic band. "The masses have been duped by capitalist propaganda and we've got to have a revolution."

"You think the masses want a revolution? All I see is people buying their houses and raising their families and arguing about Spain or Greece for their vacation."

"Yeah. They been duped with material things. That's why we got to start the revolution now. Mogens says when the conditions are right for armed struggle, it'll be too late to prepare for it."

"What does that mean?"

She blinked at me, an intruder in her two-dimensional world. "Well, it means we got to start the revolution right away and not hang around arguing. Ulrike says arguing is for the politicians and revolution is for the people. It's up to us to start the armed struggle."

"Using Simone for the shield?"

"Look, we don't want to kill her. You're the killers. Fascists like you murder people every day. It's your imperialist system that murders people. Anyway, what's murder?"

"Killing a nine-year-old girl."

"You shut your fucking mouth."

"Cathy, that girl. When you hold the Schmeisser to her head, think of all the good your revolution is doing her."

"What's with you? Stop trying to order me around. What are you anyway, a fucking Leo or something, trying to boss me?"

Cathy stood by the bed, twin spots of red in her cheeks, but still no lines of anger or doubt showing. She opened her mouth to say something more and changed her mind. She was half way to the door when I spoke again.

"Cathy, I need to go to the toilet."

"You piss in the bed."

"It's not that."

"Oh, Jesus, hell." She stopped at the door, considering. "Okay, hang in there, I'll be back."

It was Yussif she came back with. He held his Browning 9 mm Automatic on me while Cathy struggled with the knots. She untied my ankles and the cord that linked my arms to the head-rail, leaving my wrists still bound.

"I'm not wiping you," Cathy said. "You do the best you can."

The door to the toilet was left ajar and she stood where she could see I didn't stand on the seat and try for the window. Yussif stayed on sentry duty down the corridor.

When we got back to my room, she shackled my wrists to the headrail. She left the ankles. Yussif watched my face the whole time.

They left, the door closing softly on Yussif's eyes.

I heard the footfall in the corridor. I thought it must be van Berkel returning to accuse me of working for the Sûreté Nationale, even though I hadn't heard the step at the top of the stairs creak.

It was Yussif who came through the door. He had the Browning in his hand. I searched his face for the look of the executioner there. But it wasn't that.

He had come to rape me.

CHAPTER NINETEEN

LOOSDRECHTSCHE PLASSEN
FRIDAY 23 MARCH
9.10 A.M.

Then it began.

Reason says you can struggle no harder but you bloody well can. The body always responds to that most fundamental instinct: survival. My legs scissored and my arms hit out and pulled back, muscles screaming with the effort. The worst was still to come. I had only another thirty seconds at the outside, twenty, five.

The instant I heard the engine note change I flipped over on my back, exhausted, red lights probing my brain, arms and legs in agony, heart racing, pain deep inside my chest as my lungs pumped with desperation to make good the oxygen deficiency.

The ripples spread out on the surface of the lake, a couple of dozen rings with my body pinpointed at the centre and it would be the best part of a minute before they subsided. Until then I was as blatant as a target on a radar screen.

God almighty, there'd be radar in the helicopter and I hadn't considered that. No time, nothing I could have done anyway.

I had time now but the buzz alarm in my brain obliterated thought until I had to scream inside my skull: *DON'T PANIC*.

Better. Reasoning took over: aircraft radar is intended to pick out other aircraft in the sky; ground-attack radar may or may not pick out targets at ground level; no helicopter is equipped with anything to pick out a human body in a lake for the simple reason that anything so sensitive would be a jumble of irrelevant information.

I lay still in the water, watching the helicopter rise behind Wittehuis. It was an Alouette, French manufacture, seven seater. It was broadside on to me, no more than three or four hundred metres distant, and I could make out two figures in the front seats. One would be Mogens, the pilot. The other would be Vratko or Ulrike, either would be good with a sub-machine gun.

It wouldn't be Yussif in the helicopter.

I began to shiver because of the iciness of the water, and the idea of Ulrike on look-out through the open portal of the helicopter with one finger hooked inside the trigger-guard, but mostly because images of Yussif returned no matter how often I wiped the slate clean.

Yussif hadn't spoken when he came into the bedroom. He'd made an insignificant wet noise as if he were clearing his throat and gestured with his gun hand. His lips had been parted in his excitement, half grin of anticipation, half grimace at his power over me. Words could not have made his intention more explicit: he held power in his hand and power in his loins.

He clicked the door behind him, fumbling at his back while he stared at me, located the key and turned it. He made the noise in his throat again and the grin was more pronounced.

I lay on my back, focussing on his face, but only for a few instants because I'd learned from the shape of his mouth every-thing that was in his mind.

He stopped a couple of paces from the bed.

I switched to watching his hands because that would add to his excitement, and a brain that is fevered has a red curtain that stops it thinking clearly. He fumbled with the belt and then the zip of his jeans, finding it difficult because he still held the pistol in his right hand.

I knew it had to be now. There was no question of waiting for a better opportunity, pistol or not. Downstairs was Ulrike and she might have spoken to someone in Paris and this might be the last opportunity. How could I tell?

They could have summoned Yussif into the room. Van Berkel would have turned aside, hands twining together behind his back, washing themselves of responsibility, while Ulrike spoke with dead eyes. *Go upstairs. Take the gun with you and shoot the fascist pig-woman because we have learned she has been treating with the enemy. One moment: don't shoot her straight away. Let her know the end is coming. Use her body and while you do it, whisper into her ear—I'm going to shoot, I'm going to shoot into your body. Hold the pistol close against her temple the whole time. And when you have done, pull the trigger.*

I lay there, listening to the roar in my head, wanting to fight, twist, scream, scratch, bite.

I lay there on the bed, turning not away but towards him, making use of my body, and he took another step.

A man's voice floated up from outside, a new voice, it would be Mogens, and he said: "It's good, *ja?* Ufi has the fuel ready at Delfzijl and we reach Copenhagen by six."

There was some answer, I couldn't catch the words.

"Where is he?" Mogens again.

The soft voice spoke, words indistinguishable, but the rising intonation at the end made it sound like Cathy.

And Mogens laughed.

I said: "I've never had an Arab before."

Yussif had dropped his jeans to the floor and he looked at me, uncertain for a moment how to take the remark.

I was a cheap actress in a tawdry movie. I breathed through an open mouth, my chest swelled, my chin tilted up, my eyes looked through gauze at him.

"I had a friend who said they were the best. *My Arab stallion,* she called her man."

It was the red curtain that stopped him thinking. He glanced down at himself.

"Kiss me, Yussif." I put a smile on my lips.

Outside Mogens said: "I'm going to fill her up. Help me bring the cans over."

Yussif's face was suddenly serious. "Oh no, baby, I'm no fool. I kiss you and you bite my tongue off." It was only the second time I'd heard his voice.

My wrists had been tied in front of my body, with the cord going up past my shoulder to the headrail. My hands rested on my belly. I beckoned with a finger. "I didn't mean kiss my mouth."

He paused, quite motionless, while he took that in.

I heard a thin whistle on the morning air, "Yellow Submarine". There were footsteps on the gravel, the purring of doves in a tree.

The grin reappeared and Yussif unhooked the top of my slacks and unzipped them and put his hands under my buttocks to unclothe me. The material slithered across my skin and he made the wet noise in his throat again.

"Hey baby, you're sexy."

I said: "I'm hot. Just try."

I thought he'd never do it. He kneeled on the bed and I thought, he had orders not to do it. *Make sure she has no chance. Use her body but she must be disposed of afterwards. Take no risks. Hold the gun on her at all times.*

I wriggled.

Finally he laid the pistol on the floor by the bed and his tinted glasses beside it. He ran his tongue over his lips and I breathed heavily through my mouth. He bent his head over me and it was now.

There was a fraction of a second when the red curtain that had closed over his brain was ripped aside and he saw what was coming and started a reflex jerk to one side, but the blade-edge of both hands caught him under the ear and he grunted.

Through the red curtain all he had seen was what he'd wanted to see and that was my body. My wrists were bound but my ankles hadn't been retied and in the brief period before I'd caught the sound outside my door there had been time to manoeuvre myself to the headrail and unpick the knot that Cathy had tied. It had been a clumsy knot, fashioned by a child's fingers.

He slumped across my thighs, not unconscious but dazed. You can develop no power when your wrists are bound together and I had struck too much to one side of his neck. I had two seconds', three seconds' advantage, for his brain would clear quickly as it registered the signs of danger. I shifted his weight from my legs and rolled across the bed and we both arrived on the floor at the same time, with his gun knocked aside and skating across uncarpeted floor-boards under the bed.

Yussif concentrated on me because I was the prize, the possession. He gripped me round a foot and hauled me out from under the bed and found himself staring into the black eye of the Browning.

He didn't raise his hands in the air because he was not prepared to submit. He twisted with vicious strength at my leg, trying to overturn me and with no more than a metre between us I shot him. I shot him without aiming, just how the gun was pointing, at his chest. I shot without hesitation, with no agonizing about morality, though I'm not a violent person. I shot him because we were together on the jungle floor and the law of the jungle is survival. The red stained his shirt. He opened his mouth to shout but the blood bubbled out and he seemed so surprised he dropped my foot and wiped at it. He whimpered something in Arabic and wiped at the blood again.

He crawled away from me, making for the door, and the reaction started within me. Even in the few seconds since I had pulled the trigger the jungle had receded and all the doubts of civilization had welled up.

I knew with absolute certainty that I couldn't let him reach the door and call for help. They were cold-blooded. They had shot Desnos and de Groot and Sarasini. I watched Yussif crawl for ten seconds while the dark purple rising inside me said there was no difference between what they had done and what I had to do.

I followed the blood trail after him. "Don't try for the door."

I raised the pistol.

"Yussif."

He stopped crawling. I stood over him, the gun pointing at his head, and then lowering to my side. He supported himself on his knees and one hand, the other hand clasped to the lightning that struck through his chest. There were words inside him that he wanted to get out and couldn't. He stumbled over on his side, his head knocking against a chair leg.

He sighed, the breath going out of him, the muscles in his face relaxed, and he looked smaller, already less than a man.

I stared for a long time, five seconds that stretched to eternity, and slowly I turned aside and wiped the death's head from my mind.

A gunshot is a strange thing. The noise coming from half a block away can sound shockingly loud. Yet in a solid old house it can sound indistinct, diminished in importance, because the rooms and walls form primitive but effective sound baffles. To Ulrike and van Berkel downstairs it might appear no more than a door slamming.

I went to the window and to the right there was the glimpse of a rotor blade and a portion of plexiglass dome and Cathy and the pilot Mogens were standing still, staring in the direction of the house. The sound of the shot had carried through the open air and they were wondering about its significance. Mogens spoke to Cathy and I lost sight of them as they moved towards the back of the house.

I wouldn't have long.

I used the pistol butt on the glass of the window and it left a jagged edge as it shattered. It was no longer important if the sound carried. The only important thing was severing the cord that shackled my hands.

There was blood on my wrists: I only just missed the vein.

I left the gun. I left the little girl I'd come for. The one would be useless, the other an encumbrance. I left having failed, with the need merely to survive now paramount.

I dropped from the window down on to gravel, knees bent and into a forward roll and up and away past the concrete pillbox to the lakeside where Sarasini had tied the boat. Nobody shouted, nobody shot, but I only had minutes.

The mainland shore was safety and it all depended on whether the minds of the hunter and the hunted ran along the same course. They would expect me to take the shortest distance and I rowed the boat to the left where a promontory of land jutted into the lake. Still no sound of pursuit.

There were too many variables I couldn't know: Cathy and Mogens getting into the house, querying Ulrike, shouting for Yussif, checking the girl's room, getting no reply from my room, breaking down the locked door and discovering Yussif's body. Would they search the island, take out a boat, or go straight for the helicopter?

There was still no pursuit when I dropped the oars, stripped off my sweater and hurled it towards the shore. It floated, about twenty metres away.

I did a shallow dive from the boat and struck out from the promontory in a fast six-beat crawl, stopping when the sound of the helicopter warned me that pursuit had started. I floated on my back, watched as it rose high enough to clear the trees and hovered for some seconds, an ugly predatory insect: and then its tail swung and it moved off.

They had sighted the dinghy.

The Alouette clattered over in the forward pitch attitude and dipped until its wheels almost touched the dinghy. All they'd see would be the shoes I had left in the bottom of the boat last night. The Alouette edged over to my sweater and I could only hope the direction I had thrown it, towards the promontory, was suggestive.

I breathed deeply, ventilating the lungs fully, because my body had burned up oxygen and there was excess carbon dioxide in the bloodstream.

It was time I had a piece of luck.

The helicopter moved towards shore and I knew that was where their eyes would be and I took the opportunity to move further away, sidestroke, no splash and I could keep them in view. I was no longer so worried about the ripple formation I made because the turbulence from the rotor had disturbed the surface of the lake and its mirror-calm was broken as far as my position.

The promontory was covered in reeds, brown and withered after the winter. They spread out along the edge of the lake and the helicopter moved slowly away from me, the downdraught from the rotor beating the reeds while they searched for a cowering naked body.

I made another seventy or eighty metres before they turned and I had to be still.

They started towards me.

I was hyperventilating now.

When the blood suffers oxygen-starvation the brain receives the message and signals the lungs to breathe more rapidly and deeply. Even when enough oxygen has washed into the system, adrenalin can keep the lungs over-reacting because it is part of the body's preparation for sudden explosive effort.

I was going to make no explosive effort, but still I forced deep breaths.

During the Virginia training it was a sergeant from the Marines who took swimming instruction. After wetsuit and snorkel, sprint and distance, night and shallow diving, he gave instruction in Drown Proofing and Advanced Drown Proofing. To gain a credit in Drown Proofing you had to stay with your head above water for four hours; your wrists and ankles were manacled; the test was done at sea, off the Virginia coast near

Norfolk. By contrast, during Advanced Drown Proofing you had to be able to maintain yourself underwater for twelve minutes, only surfacing four times for breath. Nobody in my intake gained a credit in ADP. Two had to be hospitalized because the basic technique is dangerous. I managed better than eight minutes and then was penalized for exceeding the six seconds allowed on the surface for ventilating.

I force-breathed, flushing the carbon dioxide out of my bloodstream, and as the Alouette made its approach I sculled below surface with my hands and maintained my depth with minimal movement. Any effort burns up oxygen and can also lead to eddies on the surface.

At first I was oxygen-giddy and there was no desire whatever to breathe.

I heard the thrum of the engine as the Alouette tracked in.

I was counting into the seventies before I felt any need to breathe again.

By the mid-nineties it was painful.

At one hundred and eight I stopped hand-sculling and surfaced my face and the Alouette was a couple of hundred metres off and closing. Mogens was on my side holding course and height, looking out of the portal, face screwed up by the sun.

I managed four breaths before going under.

There was no more I could do except wait. The last of the morning mist clung to the water in wispy patches but it was no more concealing than the seventh veil. It depended on chance, whether their eyes caught some movement as my body gleamed pale through the water, whether sun reflections distracted them, how often they looked away to the island or scanned the reeds along the shore.

I counted. I forced myself to go slowly for my body was trying to cheat by speeding up the rate the numbers entered my mind, giving the false impression of time racing past.

The pain was more severe when I surfaced the second time.

The helicopter was close. Mogens was leaning across to talk to the unseen passenger and if it was to say he'd spotted me then the aft door would slide open and the Walther sub-machine gun would appear and chatter briefly and my life would stain the water of the lake.

I pushed myself below again.

The noise of the helicopter was louder and then I heard a second sound, a new rhythmic thudding that grew steadily in volume. By the time I had counted fifty I had isolated the second noise: it was my heart.

Pain was becoming a problem now because it was interfering with my mental activity and it is only by willpower that you succeed at ADP. But I am stubborn: Desnos had told me so. The pain had started in my chest where the respiratory muscles were desperate to force out the stale air and grab a fresh lungful. Now the pain had spread into my throat and shot up to my eyeballs, and there were grey and white waves of light chasing each other across my optic nerves. I opened my eyelids underwater and the waves of light flashed round in a circular motion and I wondered if I was losing consciousness and then I knew why: the helicopter was directly overhead and I had registered the flickering shadow of the rotor.

I surfaced at once. The poisoned air burst out of my lungs and I breathed deeply, again and again, tasting the sweet air, feeling the pain ebb, spluttering because I had swallowed water. The engine noise would drown my cough. Nor would they sight me because the helicopter was directly above and the solid floor of the cockpit would hide me from view.

The sky pulsed dark grey with each heartbeat and I knew my body would be unable to accept much more oxygen-starvation and the danger was I would suddenly lose control under the surface and suck in a lungful of the lake. That is the disadvantage of the ADP technique: it is those with iron wills who are most at risk.

The Alouette was stationary above me, three wheels like talons poised to plummet and grab.

Abruptly it moved away, the engine note deepening as the throttle was opened and they made a good three hundred metres before they paused again. There would be something in the water, a log, some weed. The light conditions were against them now, the sun glinting and reflecting, playing tricks.

I let the air wash into my lungs and moved with gentle strokes backwards through the water, watching the Alouette hover.

They began another sweep of the lake, further over to my left and I was no longer worried because I lay between them and the sun. All round me would be a million dancing shafts of light reflected from the water and my head would be lost among them.

It took another fifteen minutes. I touched weed and found I was in my depth and waded ashore. I burrowed like a terrified animal into the thickest of the reeds and found dry land.

I lay down, my body wracked with shakes. I was ice-cold, sodden, naked.

CHAPTER TWENTY

The man couldn't take his eyes off me.

"I want to telephone. Do you have the directory for Amsterdam?"

He went on staring.

I said: "I had an accident on the lake. The boat capsized."

He nodded and pushed the directory across the bar counter. I ordered coffee and went and sat in the corner to drink it. The café was cosy in the Dutch way, one of those warm steamy places where men take refuge from weather and wives, cream paint on the woodwork, poster for a football match in the window, radio muttering to itself, squares of carpet on the tables. I asked for a cheese *broodje* and ate slowly, washing the crumbs down with the hot milky coffee. I felt it in my stomach and like a central heating boiler it sent out warmth to my chest and arms and legs. The barman glanced in my corner because I was a curiosity in a village café, a foreign woman with gummed-down hair, wearing a man's sweater and slacks three sizes too big. No shoes. The clothes had come from one of the wooden cabins at the lakeside clearing. Money too, a handful of coins from a jam jar in the kitchen.

The Amsterdam directory listed three Poelsmas and one was *Poelsma Diamant-firma*. 020 82 74 71.

I dialled.

"Hallo."

"I want to speak with Mr Poelsma's secretary." I spoke clearly and firmly. I was an upper-class English secretary who stood no nonsense about foreign languages. Foreign languages were for the servants to speak.

"*Wilt U aan bet toestel blijven, Juffrouw?*"

I repeated my request to someone who spoke English and was connected.

"Can I help you?"

"Good morning. This is de Beers, London. I have a teeny problem."

"Who am I speaking to, please?" Her English was accented but fluent.

"Mr Stewart's secretary."

"Mr Stewart?"

"No, silly, his secretary." There was a hesitation while she was working that out and I went on. "I mean, I am speaking to the Poelsma company in Amsterdam?"

"Yes, certainly."

"Well then. Mr Stewart will be in Amsterdam this week-end and is most anxious to meet Mr Poelsma. Mr Stewart has pencilled in dinner on Saturday, if that is convenient."

"Mr Stewart?" She came back at me. "May I enquire what position this Mr Stewart holds?"

The telephone rested on a short shelf against the back of the café, with two semi-circles of thick glass to insulate the sound of the person speaking. I thought the arrangement wasn't effective. I could see the barman drying a cup, round and round with the cloth, rubbernecking on my side of the conversation, curious because I was a woman in outsize clothes with wet hair and speaking English.

"What position? How extraordinary. This Mr Stewart, as you put it, is Export Technical Director. I mean, you have after all heard of de Beers Industrial Diamond Division, London?"

"*Industrial* Division?" She made it sound as if I should be using the tradesman's entrance. "This is *Poelsma Diamant-firma*, Prinsen-gracht, you understand. You don't..."

"I'm frightfully sorry," I cut her short. "I do realize you are bangles and beads and we are the mucky side and normally I wouldn't have disturbed your calm but this is something rather out of the ordinary that came through on the teleprinter and Mr Stewart, before he left for his meeting, was most insistent, I mean he issued me explicit instructions, that I should contact Mr Poelsma wherever he was and Paris said he'd come to Amsterdam and..."

"He's not in the office at the moment."

She'd interrupted. If you talk long enough and diffusely enough they lose patience.

"At the moment, you say. He's not in the office at the moment?"

"No, he's away. And I can't speak for his private diary over the week-end."

"Oh quite, I do see that." I picked at what she'd said. "But still, Mr Stewart will be able to contact him this week-end? I mean Mr Poelsma is returning from wherever it is?"

"Yes, I made the return reservation for today."

"Now why couldn't your Paris people have been helpful like you and told me he'd flown to New York?"

"Not New York," she said. "Tel Aviv."

Ask a straight question and you run into a brick wall. But she didn't often have the chance of correcting someone and it made her feel superior.

I said: "Marvellous, thank you. That's the two o'clock arrival from Tel Aviv, if memory serves me correctly."

"Yes. Two thirty-five to be precise."

"Most helpful. Mr Stewart will be in touch."

I rang off as two people came through the door and I checked because it was possible that Blood Group O would widen the search. The men wore overalls with "Shell" on the breast pocket. They shook hands with the bartender and glasses were filled at the beer-tap. Their tanker darkened the windows. Fuel for the central heating.

Something snagged inside my brain. There was some connection I should be making.

I fetched a second cup of coffee, all three men watching as I padded back to my table. I lowered my head and let the drifting steam bathe some of the tiredness out of my face.

The time underwater was still slowing me: oxygen-starvation impairs the brain. Or was it the lack of sleep? Or was I growing old?

Then I squeezed my eyes tight because my brain made the connection. It had been too big for me to take in before. An ant is pre-occupied with climbing up a step and never sees the Empire State Building beyond.

I was staring at the clock on the wall. Old, with a mottled face and brass numbers. 11.18.

"No, I don't know the number. You'll have to find it for me."

The International operator was patient. He was patient even when I told him the call was going to be collect, because I didn't have enough coins. He was still patient when the Sûreté Nationale demurred at picking up the tab.

"They want to know who's calling?"

"On behalf of Chief Inspector Crevecoeur," I told him.

I held the receiver away from my head. You do that with a Paris exchange because it can hurt the eardrums when they make the connection.

The clock on the wall showed 11.29.

When I got through to the switchboard at rue des Saussaies she was going like popcorn in a fryer.

"It is highly irregular. I shall require mademoiselle's name and address. More—I shall require evidence of authority." She had dentures that clacked her disapproval. "To make an international call and not have the money… It is the taxpayers' money, you see?"

That only worries them when it is a taxpayer who tries to get something in return.

I gave my name and address.

"But I was told the call was from a café in some place called Middeldorp in the Netherlands."

"Correct."

"What is the name of the café?"

"Is Chief Inspector Crevecoeur available?"

"No, mademoiselle, he is not."

"It is imperative I speak to him."

"That is not possible."

So it went.

It was 11.36 when I was connected to someone in Crevecoeur's *bureau*.

"My name is Cody. I don't know whether the Chief Inspector has kept you fully informed about me."

The French pride themselves on their logic. The rest of the world says they are pedantic.

"Mlle Cody, I am not able to say whether Chief Inspector Crevecoeur has kept us fully informed. There may be things he has not discussed. I simply cannot tell." His voice was slow, accustomed to filling out every statement in triplicate. "But we are aware that you went to discuss a certain matter with him at Château-Franqui on Wednesday evening."

"I need to speak to him."

"I regret, mademoiselle, we are not allowed to divulge classified information on the telephone. The Chief Inspector's whereabouts is classified. Especially to a foreigner."

"It is in connection with the matter I discussed with him on Wednesday."

"Possibly. That is not for me to judge. It is for the Chief Inspector."

"But if I can't speak to him, how can he judge it?"

"Precisely."

Every country suffers from bureaucracy. But it is no accident we take the word from the French.

"Who am I speaking to?" I asked.

"Sergeant Duclos."

"Who is your immediate superior?"

"Inspector Tourneclef."

"I would like to speak ... "

"I regret the Inspector is in conference."

"Then the Commissioner."

"To speak to the Commissioner, you should make an application in writing."

And so I tried the long shot, the throw in the dark, while he still felt self-satisfied at thwarting me.

"When did they switch the President's arrival in Amsterdam from Sunday to today?"

"You are mistaken," he said. "The Sunday arrival was always a cover. The true arrangements ... " He ran out of self-satisfaction. "How did you acquire that information? It has the highest classification."

I hung up. 11.44 showed on the clock.

Some elect to be soldiers. Some to be city cops. For them it is the thrill of having a human adversary.

But there are others, our kind.

Crevecoeur had recognized in me a fellow-sufferer: he knew the secret passion that excites us. It is heady, like the first days of a love affair, when every action is touched with magic. It comes from doing something unknown, more outrageous than anything the rest of humankind can conceive. It is because of the edge of danger and because it stretches every fibre of your being. And while the fuse burns down, the adrenalin mounts and you remember why it was you got involved in the first place, why you underwent four years in Virginia. Yes, and why you had to get out, because it was something so private and you couldn't do it with a committee in Langley watching on.

And so I had become involved, as Crevecoeur understood I had to. Not just because of Desnos or the little girl. They were part of the pattern, out at the edge. At the centre was Blood Group O and what they intended. The situation existed, hidden from the rest of the world, and begged to be played with.

It's a game we play, isn't it? Crevecoeur's words in my Paris apartment had lodged in my memory. *A game like chess. We know chess isn't life. But once one gets involved, one wants to win the game. No, not wants, has to win, a compulsion.*

That was me. The very heart of me.

A little cold coffee was left in the second cup. I drank it gratefully.

I knew it now. The when and the where and the who. Just not the how.

Enquiries gave me the number of the French embassy in The Hague.

I asked for the Legal Department.

"Chateau-Franqui switchboard," I announced. I concentrated on getting an unemotional north French accent. "I have a call for Chief Inspector Crevecoeur."

I heard the click. The Dutch telephone system isn't like that so it would be the recording device.

"One moment, if you please," he said. "No, nobody of the name Crevecoeur works at the embassy."

"He's attached."

"I'm sorry."

Normal procedure.

I said: "It's all right. We have full clearance."

"Will you identify, please."

I said: "SN." I sighed at the tedium of it.

There was a hesitation. There was bound to be. I hadn't got it right because I didn't know their verbal code-intro.

He said: "Give me your number. I'll call you."

I said: "For God's sake, you know and I know that Chief Inspector Crevecoeur is not at this moment in your embassy building. We know that because of the importance of the work he is doing this afternoon. I need to contact him and it is far too urgent for international telephone delays. No," I finished, half-cupping the mouthpiece, "they are playing children's games in The Hague. It truly is too much."

"You maintain that you are the switchboard at Château-Franqui?"

"I have security. All this morning I have been occupied with this affair."

"Who wishes to speak to the Chief Inspector?"

"Inspector Tourneclef of the Chief Inspector's *bureau*. You may confirm if you feel you have to."

"One instant."

I watched the clock crawl to 11.59. Two minutes.

He said: "You must contact the Maison Culturelle Française in Amsterdam."

"Hasn't he left for the airport yet?"

"It is not necessary. Touchdown isn't until eighteen hours."

For a moment it threw me. Then I realized I'd made a wrong assumption. The President of France wasn't the big apple. He wasn't who Blood Group O was after.

The Shell tanker had left. Four men played cards at one of the tables. A young man and woman were dunking bread into bowls of thick pea soup. The door opened and two mechanics in grease-stained dungarees came in for a beer.

I had to ask for the Amsterdam directory again and I sat at my table, searching for the number, paying no attention when the door opened because it was getting busy round lunchtime, and I heard her humming "Yellow Submarine".

"Don't try anything," she said. She stood close behind and had seen my neck stiffen. "I have a grenade. Pin's out, thumb on the lever."

"You're bluffing," I said.

"Suit yourself."

"I'm going to turn round, very slowly, and you're going to show it to me."

Cathy wore a bomber jacket over her T-shirt and had her right hand in one pocket, clasped to her belly. She let me see. It was dark grey, seemed almost too big for her hand. Her fingernails were bitten down to the quick.

"You must understand that a grenade is final, know what I mean?" Cathy's voice was earnest, as if she were instructing a child. "With a revolver there's a chance I'd miss. With a grenade, I'm certain. That's what Ulrike said."

"But you'd kill yourself," I pointed out. "That's also certain."

"Sure. Requires commitment," she answered. "You are a tool of the imperialists and you have lost your faith. I believe one thousand per cent in what Blood Group O is doing. I believe strongly enough to make the ultimate sacrifice. Can you understand? You must grasp that the struggle means everything to me, the success of the revolution is more important than an individual life. The struggle is necessary and in the context of history I am already dead." A grin bobbed on her face. "I do hope you see that."

I knew it was hopeless but when death is standing by your shoulder you're a fool not to try everything.

I looked round the café. I think the four men were playing bridge. One was slapping his cards down, peeved with his partner. Nobody watched us.

"But you'd murder all these people."

"Oh, the innocents," she said.

CHAPTER TWENTY-ONE

LOOSDRECHTSCHE PLASSEN
FRIDAY 23 MARCH
12.20 P.M.

"Pay."

I beckoned to the barman.

"Be real careful what you say."

The barman was using a small wooden paddle to scoop foam from the top of a glass of beer. He pushed the glass across the counter, wiped his hands on a towel, ducked under a flap at the end of the bar, walked over to us. I used the time to review my options: I could say something to the barman; I could knock Cathy down and trust to be quick enough to chuck the grenade outside; I could pay and leave with her.

We turned left into the village street and she had the hired BMW parked a little way down. They would have searched Sarasini's body for papers and turned up the Avis key-ring. I'd had to hitch a lift the five kilometres into Middeldorp.

She tossed the keys to me.

"You drive," she said. "I've got to nurse this thing." She clutched the hand to her body.

We sat a moment in the car. The sky in Holland is immense, throwing a big light across everything, a flat light, a painter's light. Cathy's face shone in the light, innocence in her smile.

"There'd have been problems if you couldn't drive."

I'd thought of that.

I'd thought of sprinting down the main street: you can make a lot of ground in eight seconds with the thought of that thing bouncing along the paving behind you. But it might not be an eight-second fuse: it might only be a three-second delay. Also, the human arm can hurl faster than human legs can run.

I'd thought of the police station. A place this size would have one. I'd dismissed the thought. The police would be attuned to different problems, would stare with open faces as I tried to convey a sense of urgency. "A hand grenade, Juffrouw? What would anyone want with a hand grenade in our nice little town of Middeldorp?"

I'd thought because thoughts were my only weapon.

"You are going to be careful?" she asked, concerned at the silence.

"Where are we heading—the airport?"

"You know so much, don't you," she said. And added with a spurt of venom, "Too bloody much, you dirty police spy."

So they'd heard from Paris.

I sat with my hands on the wheel, staring straight ahead, waiting for calm to come to her.

"Drive back to the lake, where you dumped the car in the first place."

I turned the key.

A young woman crossed the street in front of us, pushing a pram, trailing another kid in a junior version of a boiler suit. The boy tumbled over, his ball rolling under the car. He started bawling, and his mother slapped him which made it worse. And we sat in the car, waiting. Cathy was very tense. We waited while the mother wheeled the pram to the pavement, dusted down the boy, bent to retrieve the ball from under a front wheel. The mother spoke something to us, an apology. We sat like Mount Rushmore.

"Come on, get going."

I took it slowly going out of the village and she said: "Come on, don't drag it out."

We were passing the big greenhouses. No good. Glass was no protection.

An Amstel beer truck overtook us and she said: "Holy cow, you're slow."

"What's the rush? Poelsma's not due in until 2.35."

At the edge of vision I could see she shifted on the seat to stare at me. She didn't query the relevance of Poelsma.

Ahead was the line of electricity pylons marching across ploughed fields. No good. I needed a farm building, a solid barn with an open door, anything with the possibility of swinging off the road and slamming into; anything that gave a chance of blocking her grenade.

"Where's Mogens?"

"Other way up the road."

"And the others, are they looking?"

"Shut up."

Two of Blood Group O were dead and their operation had hardly got into the countdown time. It worried her and she was taut.

"What happens when we reach the lake?"

"Goddam shut up and drive, right?"

It would happen when we reached the wooden cabins, or when we were on the lake, or when we'd returned to the island. There was no telling but it would happen soon because with two killed there weren't enough of them left to guard me and anyway why should they bother now? I was no threat dead. I thought Cathy would wait for Mogens to return and Mogens would have a pistol, and a gun would be less dangerous than a grenade. A grenade makes a hell of a bang and shreds of hot metal go all over, but a pistol might be someone out duck-shooting.

Hut on the left but its door was shut and might be locked. I hadn't put on the seatbelt and if I rammed the door we might both catapult into the windscreen. No good ending up groggy and unable to crawl free before the blast.

And after Mogens and Cathy returned to the island they'd load the sub-machine guns into the helicopter and fly to the airport because there were a lot of Heads of State flying in during the afternoon. A helicopter sweeping in low would give the security forces a hell of a surprise. At 180 kph they'd hedgehop the perimeter fence and within twenty seconds be directly over the red carpet area and then away while Crevecoeur and Duraine and all the security men with dark glasses and walkie-talkies were running in small circles.

That wasn't it. I still didn't know how.

Poelsma was part of it, returning from Tel Aviv at 2.35, and how did he fit?

It would be Poelsma who'd known the Summit arrivals were timed for Friday not Sunday, because of his links with the Sûreté Nationale.

"There's the turn-off."

Down to the right was the thick belt of reeds at the edge of the lake and beyond, which I hadn't been able to see in the dark, was the water dirtied by a midday breeze. I could even make out the big willow trees and the roof of the house on the island.

The track was untarred but smooth, curving down to the reeds and the wooden cabins, no more than four or five hundred metres.

It was going to be close to suicide and I pushed the thought away.

I didn't like it. I had made up my mind because it was the only thing I could do now but still there were three distinct ways I could be killed in about forty seconds' time. They were possibilities and I would risk them because if I waited quietly for the return of Mogens my death would be a certainty.

Cathy gripped the grenade, hunching over it, peering through the window to see if Mogens had come back.

As the car entered the reeds I put it to her directly not because I anticipated an answer but to distract her attention.

"Poelsma isn't a real member of Blood Group O. Tell me what his part is."

She hunched herself round on the seat and I think for the first time a frown disturbed her face. I kept probing at the nasty surprise Blood Group O was planning.

Her tone was querulous. "Why do you keep asking? What difference does it make to you?"

She was intent on me, not looking out of the car. She couldn't understand me. She could understand how to snap the pin out of a grenade and how to squeeze the trigger on a gun. I was something else.

If she had understood me, she would never have let me drive. The person behind the wheel has the initiative. But I'd had the Virginia training and she hadn't. She was only a kid who knew it all.

She didn't notice the engine note change as I put my foot down because she was still absorbed by my query. Then we were in the final run and it happened too fast for her to react. I blessed Sarasini's insecurity, that he'd craved so much power under the bonnet. A blur of reeds as we burst out into the open and I swerved round a man standing holding a fishing rod. Cathy jerked her head frontwards as the car flashed between two wooden cabins and the engine note was still rising as I banged a hand on my door handle and she opened her mouth to yell something. Even if she'd lifted her thumb off the little lever, the grenade would have done nothing for her now.

I locked the wheel hard over to the right. The tyres tore at the roughness of the dirt on the mooring levee and topping 90 kph the momentum was irresistible. It was centrifugal force that snatched me out of death. Cathy was screaming as she was flung sideways across the seat, my door swinging wide open as I was propelled out into space. Flecks of sunlight were dancing on the lake as I separated from the car and we both dived towards the water.

CHAPTER TWENTY-TWO

LOOSDRECHTSCHE PLASSEN
FRIDAY 23 MARCH
12.55 P.M.

He was kissing me.

He was bent over my face, the sun shining gold in his curls. He hadn't shaved that morning and I felt the rough masculine rasp of him against my cheek.

He had no name. His mouth was on mine, fingers on my chin and nose, and I didn't know him.

My chest convulsed and I coughed, choking, wanting to vomit and he sat back on his haunches.

"*Voorzichtig, Juffrouw, voelt U zich goed?*"

Perhaps I had known him, very long ago, in my dreams, dreams playing tricks with my life, slipping forward to visit the future, crazy.

"What?" My brain was fuddled.

Fear stabbed at me. This strange man who was not quite strange had been kissing me and I was lying on the ground and above me there were sun and cottonwool clouds in the blue. I had no recollection of going to sleep. I remembered nothing. Where was I? I turned my head and the ground dipped and rocked to the crazy rhythm in my head. Spiky withered stems of reeds throbbed. I turned the other way and it came flooding back.

Memory blanks out and it is terrifying to be conscious and to know nothing: where you are, what has happened.

Now I knew I wasn't insane: the world was, that part of it I was in.

I saw the lake flecked with sunlight and the island with the white-painted house and there, in the water in front of me, was the wavering shape of the car and sticking out like a reed was its radio aerial.

I moved and he said: "Be careful. You're American too?"

"What happened to her?"

"Your friend? She got out of the car. She was lucky not to be trapped. It's not easy to push a door open against water. Remember Chapaquiddick."

I sat up straight, the pain in my head beating to the pumping of my heart. I raised a hand and felt and my hand was wet, mainly water, a thin smear of red. My clothes were soaking too.

"Where's she gone?"

"She went back to the road to look for help."

Meaning Mogens.

"She was luckier than you really. You knocked your head against the marker-buoy going into the lake. You took in quite a bit of water."

I was trying to stand. So little time.

"Easy," he said. He had a deep voice, Dutch, but no hesitation with the English words. He put an arm round my shoulder. "What happened? Did the brakes fail?"

"Something like that."

I inspected him. I had seen him before, a millisecond as the car flashed past, holding a fishing rod. His hair was a mad confusion, bleached by the sun, his eyes intense blue against the tan of his face. The grip on my shoulders was hard.

"Come inside. You can't stay like that, you're soaking."

His wooden cabin was next door to the one I'd broken into. It was a summer place, with thin boards that wouldn't keep out the cold, rattan furniture, tennis rackets, fishing tackle, waterskis, a

DAVID BRIERLEY

portable wheeled barbecue. There were withered flowers in a jug, a stopped clock, gaps in the bookshelf.

"I've got some clothes you can borrow. They're only cast-offs, about your size. They belonged to a friend."

Past tense noted. She was no longer here. I didn't want to involve innocent strangers because to Blood Group O there were no innocents. I pushed open the shutters and listened. No car, no boat, no helicopter, no voice. How long had I been out?

He showed me the closet and I struggled into a matelot sweater and denim slacks with paint stains on them. The scuffed tennis shoes were a size too large because Dutch women's feet aren't doll-like, but I wasn't complaining.

He'd gone into the kitchen and I was tying the laces when they came back. So soon.

I heard the engine noise and the tyres scattering stones and through the net curtains I saw a shiny red VW Passat pull up at the mooring levee. Cathy and Mogens stood at the water's edge, looking at the drowned car, and then did a 360-degree turn, searching. Their eyes were greedy for me.

I heard the rattle of a spoon in a saucer and I was into the kitchen very fast before my benefactor with the curly hair could shout through the window.

He said, "Your friend has found help. I'll make another … "

"She's not a friend."

He shrugged as if I were quibbling: friend, acquaintance, cousin, hitch-hiker. He turned his head to look through the kitchen window. His face was square, tufts of eyebrows bleached, wrinkles in his forehead with no white in the depths. He'd been a long time in the sun, more than a pale Dutch winter sun.

"What's your name?"

"Joop Prinsloo."

"Joop, I haven't time to explain, and you might not believe me if I did … "

He swung his head back. I was displaying signs of dementia, delayed shock, another spasm of amnesia: his face mirrored his thoughts. I took a step into the kitchen to bring the people outside into view. They had their heads bent: there was a wet patch on the ground where my body had lain.

"Can you accept they are not my friends? They're nobody's friends. They're extremely dangerous. They..."

The kettle stopped me. It had a shrill whistle and I saw Cathy and Mogens turn towards the noise and start over.

"Joop, tell them I've left."

The tan of his face made his eyes piercing blue. They were outdoor eyes, accustoming to fixing on the sky or the horizon, and perhaps the brain behind wasn't geared to quick decisions.

"Who are you?" he asked.

"Joop, believe me, they are killers."

I had to leave it. I retreated and fitted myself behind a rack of clothes in the closet.

I saw nothing. I could hear. Shoes on the plank steps, the kitchen door opening.

"Where is she?" Cathy asked, very abrupt. "The British woman?" She had the same phrasing Ulrike had, referring to me as an "American woman". Cathy was American herself: this was a form of denial.

"You mean your friend?" Joop asked.

"Yes, my friend. Where is she?"

"She's gone."

The kettle moaned and died.

"Who's that for?"

"I was making coffee for you."

"Why the extra cup?"

"Stop wasting time, Cathy. You look in there, I'll..."

"Hold on a minute." Joop's voice had a rasp to it. "You can't go breaking into my house."

"We're looking for our friend," Mogens said.

"You know her too?"

"Stop asking questions all the time."

"Hey." It was Cathy's voice, from just outside the closet. I hadn't heard her move because she was light and I'd been listening to the voices. "Here are her wet clothes."

"All right, is she bloody hiding here?"

"I told you, she's gone."

There were steps on the wooden boards and a jolt as a body was pressed against the closet door. I could hear breathing, they were that close.

"We're in a hurry. Our friend is a tiny bit crazy and we got to find her."

"Perhaps the British woman never left," Cathy said. "Let me take a look..."

I had my foot braced against the back of the closet. Cathy's grenade was lost in the lake but Mogens would have a gun. Assumption: he had it out, pressed under Joop's chin. If the closet door opened I would use what element of surprise I had, bursting out like a gamebird put up by the dogs. My fist gripped one of the wire hangers. From the sound of his voice I positioned Mogens's face: the loop of the hanger had a sharp end and I would go for the eyes.

"She left." Joop's voice was flat, very calm. "She was in a great hurry, running."

"*Come on*," Mogens shouted. "Which way did she go?"

"There's a path to the left that leads to the boat club. I told her it was closed until Easter but she went anyway. She took a knife."

"Bitch." Mogens's voice had moved away towards the kitchen. "Cathy, you're wasting time."

"She could still be here. Suppose this guy is lying."

"Mister, you're not hiding anything?"

"Look around," Joop said. "I'll make coffee."

"It's not a fucking social call. Come on, Cathy."

I didn't relax. Their footfalls died and I stayed in the dark because they might return, sensing a trick. The closet door opened and Joop said: "What happens when they find you didn't go along the lake?"

His voice was steady. I thought there was some red under the tan of his face.

"Did he have a gun?"

Joop stood four-square with his feet apart. He was scowling as he rubbed his stomach.

"I told you they weren't my friends," I said.

"What kind of people are they?"

"Do you have a phone?"

"In the kitchen. You want the police?"

"Sort of."

"The nearest police bureau is Middeldorp."

"I need more than the village police."

I had the kitchen window open so I'd have warning of Cathy and Mogens's return. I could hear the cries of waterfowl and the distant sound of a diesel engine, a tractor. There was another sound, like an animal in distress, and it worried me until I'd placed it: gulls following the tractor, wheeling and swooping as the ploughshares turned up grubs.

"I'll make coffee."

"Have you any food?"

"Some sausage." He stopped by a cupboard. "I save you from drowning, give you the kiss of life, people come looking for you with a gun, and I don't know your name."

"Call me Co."

"Co? A funny sort of name."

"Yes, Joop."

He caught my look and he had a lopsided grin.

I dialled the Maison Culturelle in Amsterdam and asked for Crevecoeur.

"Who?"

"Crevecoeur, Chief Inspector, Sûreté Nationale."

Mademoiselle must comprehend that this is an institution for the wider dissemination of the achievements of French civilization etc., etc. Nothing to do with French security etc., etc. Seriously jeopardize the friendship between the French and Dutch peoples if the cultural nature of the work was compromised etc., etc.

I got the number.

My watch said 2.02 when the new sound came. I paused in dialling because I might have to duck through the front door and run very fast. It appeared from behind a reed-covered spit of land jutting into the lake and Joop and I watched. It was a speedboat, the sort that tows waterskiers and if it had banked into a right turn it could have been bumping alongside the levee in thirty seconds. It kept a straight profile. There were two figures in it. The smaller one, it would be Cathy, had her face turned towards the cabin. I stood back in the depths, against the wall.

"Heading for the island," Joop said.

I was finishing dialling the number. It was the Security headquarters, Amsterdam airport, that answered.

"Will you connect me with Chief Inspector Crevecoeur."

"Which agency, please?" The girl used English, as I had.

Jesus. It's a small country and a quarter of it would sink beneath the waves if they let the sea loose. Nobody's going to learn their language because it's not important so at school they're taught French, English and German. They were playing host to a Middle East peace conference because the world was running short of small disinterested countries that had facilities. They had the heads of six foreign governments arriving within the space of four or five hours, and every one of those foreign governments would have security people crawling out of the woodwork, checking files, vetting photographs, muttering into sleeve mikes. And you ring up the Security HQ at the airport and, *Which agency*, the girl asks, *please*. So polite.

"French," I told her. It had to be Crevecoeur: he was my contact and he'd have the clout to organize a security sweep even though it wasn't the French President who was threatened.

And he wasn't there.

I couldn't believe it. This was the big day, not only Crevecoeur's own President but the other Western leaders and he wasn't there.

"Can I connect you with someone else?"

The speedboat had creamed to a halt at the island. I could hear the tractor and the gulls again.

No good. Hopeless. No point in talking to some faceless security cop and saying: Terrorists are planning to assassinate the American President. They've developed a special yawn for that. They get two dozen calls every time he stirs out of the White House.

"Caller, are you still there?"

I said: "The information for Chief Inspector Crevecoeur is in connection with the arrival of the President of the United States of America. What is the latest ETA?"

"Please hold." Pause. I rubbed a dirty spot on the base of the phone. The voice came back: "Still given out as 1500 hours."

"Thank you."

"You're welcome."

Joop held out a plate of Brabant sausage and dark rye bread. I was no longer hungry.

"Do you know who lives on that island?"

"Piet van Berkel," he said. "Got a holiday home. Some bigshot lawyer."

"You've met him?"

"We've said good day."

"Joop, do you know what all this is about? Aren't you curious?"

His blue eyes looked right into me.

"Perhaps I'm afraid to know."

And I understood. Usually it only happens with someone you've known a long time. He spoke shorthand but if he'd written it all out it would have gone something like this: *We've run together in strange circumstances and we know nothing about each other's lives and I'm afraid if I discover more of your affairs you may turn out to be someone I no longer like.* But half a sentence was enough.

I said: "People meet in the damnedest ways, don't they?"

"Right."

There was no time for more but I said: "I'm not a gangster, I'm not a reporter, I'm not police."

"But you're not saying who you are. You see why I was afraid."

"Listen, will you? I have been pushed and duped and maybe I've been lucky but this is what I've found. On that island is a group of political terrorists with their middle-aged, middle-class sympathizer. They have planned an assassination. Now, this afternoon, in an hour, the American President arrives at Amsterdam airport. There must be five hundred or a thousand police and troops to provide security but these people have found a way to get through. Do you believe me?"

He said: "What are you, Co? Some kind of…"

"Not now."

The silence was broken by the noise from the lake and we both turned to the window.

The helicopter rose from the island, glinting in the sun's rays, and I had one hope left: that they would abort the operation, turn north and make for the Danish border, or east and head for Germany. I could see figures in the cabin, but not who or even how many. The tail swung round and even as it continued gaining altitude it moved away west.

There was only one thing to do and I didn't like it because the Passat was bright red and would stand out on the road.

"I'm taking their car," I said. If Mogens hadn't left the key in the ignition, I'd lose another half minute starting it and I didn't know how many minutes I'd got.

"You'll do better with me," Joop said, "I've got a bike."

CHAPTER TWENTY-THREE

His bike was a Yamaha 750 cc.

Joop said: "I've pushed it to 185 on the circuit, but that wasn't with two up."

After that we couldn't talk. Perhaps he lost 10 kph with me riding pillion behind him. On a long corner on the road going north from Middeldorp he was banked over so far he was scratching, the footpeg screeching against the road surface.

As we reached the filter road on to the E9 the sun was blotted out and in the same moment it began to pour. The sudden squall gusted in from the west, a violent rain. My body couldn't feel the buffets because of our own slipstream but the motorbike raced through patches of disconcerting judder. I had my face tucked in close against Joop's back to avoid the windrush.

For the second time in twelve hours I raced the helicopter but with this difference: we knew where we were headed, and because of the daylight conditions the helicopter approached its maximum speed. It cut away to the west while we had to follow the autoroute north as far as the cloverleaf before peeling off to join the highway that ran through Ouderkerk and Amstelveen and on to the airport. Joop had the kind of expertise you expect when someone has moved up to the superbike class. It's nothing like the compensation need that had made Sarasini choose

174

a big car. Joop could boss a powerful piece of machinery, seeing gaps in traffic, hunched low, goggles smeared from the rain and the muck thrown up by the heavy transports. The trucks' brakes hissed like angry snakes as we looped in front.

For the third time that day I was cold and wet, my fingers numbed.

Joop shouted, the words snatched away in the turbulence. He slowed right down and repeated: "I've lost it, lost the helicopter."

I raised my face into the wind and the horizon was empty. I swung round and the fields to the left were brilliant in unexpected sunshine. I found the helicopter and it was over on the right, framed in a rainbow that dipped down and seemed to end back where we'd come from in Loosdrechtsche Plassen. We were some two kilometres from the airport perimeter now but the helicopter had swung north and was flying parallel to the boundary.

My watch said 2.42.

"They're on our right," I told him. "They're heading north."

"Aren't they making for the airport?"

"They must be ahead of schedule. They'd want that in case the President's plane got in early."

"What are they going to do?"

"How the hell should I know?" I felt sudden anger with him, expecting me to know their plans, to be inside the minds of madmen. "They'll have radio. If they've found the frequency they'll be listening to Amsterdam Control Tower talking to the pilot."

"Just like that? Won't the radio be put through a scrambler?"

"Well then, they'll use their eyes."

The helicopter was lost to view now. It had been very low, chimney height.

We were running along the perimeter fence and two marked police cars were parked on the hard shoulder. Beyond the fence on the grass was a circle of sandbags and three or four helmets above the top. Beyond the sandbags was an abandoned half-track and beside it a mobile anti-aircraft gun. That would be for show and because it gave the army a warm glow to display its toys: it would be no use against a helicopter that came in fast at hedge-hop height. Even if they picked up the helicopter now, doing its low sweep parallel to the fence, they'd mark it as one of theirs on patrol against intruders.

We drove the length of the perimeter fence. Armed soldiers stood like statues.

They hadn't shut the airport but there were uniforms every-where. The sun came out again, winking on brass buttons like miniature heliographs.

"Well, what?"

Joop had stopped, one foot on the ground, slewing his head round to me.

"I can't involve you..." I began.

"What is it?"

There were eyes watching us and I saw an arm wave.

"The point is this, Joop." I'd given it some thought on the run from the lake. "I have to get to see someone in authority and it's no use just asking: they'll assume I've jumped over the wall of the funny farm. It's a matter of creating a diversion so they positively drag me off for questioning, which could mean an element of danger."

The one who'd waved an arm had started in our direction. He wore a dark blue uniform with breeches tucked inside black leather boots. I could hear the tapping of the metal tips of his boots above the idling throb of the Yamaha. He had motorbike cop written across his face. He was jogging forward, slow, lost without his saddle and handlebars, and he'd be malicious by the time he reached us.

Joop said: "We're wasting time."

There was the sound of tyres approaching fast from the high-way and I thought somebody else was coming up behind to take us but it curled round to the left where the barbed wire divided the forecourt from the top security area. It was large and black, an official Mercedes, and as it drew close the sentries recognized the number plate and hauled aside the gate. Somebody in khaki saluted.

The man in blue was yelling at us as he came: they like their authority to go before them.

I shouted: "Now. Through there."

In an automobile 750 cc feels like a fairground dodgem. In a motorbike it is savage. Joop had the throttle fully open and the power surging through to the rear wheel spat loose chippings out behind us as the tread struggled to find grip and the acceleration nearly kicked me off the pillion as we burned away past the cop with his mouth hideously open and his shout lost in the anger of our engine. The Mercedes was clear of the gate and we were closing fast on it before the sentries realized what was intended and one of them tried to drag the gate shut while the other struggled with the rifle that was slung behind his shoulder. The third one, the one who'd been saluting five seconds before, made a grab for the stubbynosed machine pistol he'd laid on a bench and Joop pointed the front wheel deliberately at him, and then we were through the wire and nobody could shoot because the Merc was like a big black safety curtain in front of us.

"Stop."

I hit Joop between the shoulder blades and he punched the brakes so hard the momentum thrust me half over his back. He slewed the bike round in a final skid at the same moment the driver of the Mercedes figured what was happening and swung away to the right. We came to a halt in clear space and somebody at the gate loosed off three rapid-fire shots that bit into the road a couple of metres beyond us. I bundled off the pillion and rolled on the ground until I was shoes on to the sentries, presenting the least possible target. Joop switched off the ignition, hoisted the big machine on its sidestand and stepped away, totally calm, hands in the air, calling out something in Dutch.

My cheek was pressed against wet tarmac and I heard the rush of feet and unfamiliar words of command. I didn't have to understand: the tone of voice means the same in every language. I got up with caution, keeping my hands away from my body, wiped the mud off my cheek on my shoulder. I was at the wrong end of three automatic rifles. On the roof of the passenger terminal building 150 metres away there were sharpshooters with sniperscopes on their rifles.

A soldier with large brown eyes was feeling at my clothes for anything hard underneath when I heard the sudden roar of reverse thrust from one of the parallel runways. I saw the big jet slowing. It had overshot the terminal building and would have to turn-about and come back on one of the taxiways.

The crystal on my Omega had smashed. The hands were at 2.49. The El Al flight was late.

My arm ached from the grip of the soldier's fingers but I wouldn't rub it. Not pride. I didn't want this officer to feel they had achieved any kind of power over me: everything that was going to happen in the next minutes had to undermine his feeling of authority and superiority.

The atmosphere was cloying with the honeyed smell of Clan tobacco, sharp with distrust.

"A foreigner, no papers, ignoring the orders of a police officer, breaking into a restricted area. Then you come out with a kiddies' bedtime story."

He was dressed in an olive-green uniform with red shoulder tabs. His pipe had gone out but the sickly smell lingered. The nameplate on the door had announced *Kapt. J. de Wet OOH/5.* He sat at a desk with wire in/out trays, external telephone and internal squawkbox, pens, ashtray, a dirty cup, and a neat heap of grey and fawn files of which the top one had a red star and a distribution list. Careless. I noticed de Wet's name was second on the list. When they finish with you at Virginia Training the habits are ingrained for life.

I stood in front of the desk with a security man a step behind me. Joop was detained in another room. Normal procedure. He'd be questioned separately so his story could be checked against mine for discrepancies.

"My name is Cody, I am an British citizen resident in Paris, I am an associate of Chief Inspector Crevecoeur of the French Sûreté Nationale and it is not a bedtime story, it is desperately urgent."

I'd given it to him once already while he sat taking short puffs at his pipe, holding the match to the bowl until it scorched his fingers, eyes measuring me through the cloud of grey.

"Desperately urgent," he echoed.

"International importance. You can see that." His eyes were bright and he had a huge domed forehead but I have no high regard for Military Intelligence officers except for the GRU and the Israeli Modi'in.

"You work for the Sûreté? Then where is your documentation?"

"It is co-operation with Crevecoeur personally. I am not in their employ." I looked at my watch. It still said 2.49. There was a wall clock showing 2.58. "You have very little time. Ask Crevecoeur."

It wasted a minute. Sometimes de Wet looked up at me while the switchboard girl's voice could be heard thinly making enquiries, sometimes he doodled on a pad, a tall glass with shaded liquid. I could hear footsteps in the corridor, the jangle of a phone somewhere, a man's voice raised.

"Crevecoeur is absent from their temporary office. Nobody is certain where."

"The American President is due here any minute. You must treat this as urgent."

"That information is classified high security. How did you acquire ... "

"Oh, for God's sake." They'd classify the Amsterdam streetcar routes as top security if you let them. "You have heard of Blood Group O?"

"Do you imagine we don't know our jobs? Their slogans are all over Amsterdam. We have been successful in detaining a number of agitators."

"The people who daub slogans on walls aren't the people who act," I told him. "You must have learned that. Those are just the sympathizers, the ones who enjoy feeling persecuted when the police pick them up. I'm talking about the ones who are planning this operation. The core. They know the President is coming, the time, the security arrangements. Is the plane late?"

He ruminated about it, whether it was too secret for me to know. "A little. The American liaison officer here has said it was re-timed for 3.15." He tapped his pipe in the ashtray, suddenly brisk. "What do you know of these plans? How do you know? Who is involved?"

"They have a helicopter. They are going to fly in when the President has arrived ... "

"Then there is no problem. We have six helicopters on stand-by, a squadron of Starfighters. Our forces here are overwhelming. You are wasting my time. See for yourself."

De Wet hauled himself up from behind the desk and switched on three television monitors on a wooden shelf. The sound came on at once, a curious babel of Dutch and American voices and I could pick out one of those deep dominant mid-West accents: " ... down the west runway C43H most immediate." And another voice distorted by a small radio transmitter: "Wilco, Blue Cat."

I looked out of the window before the tubes warmed up. De Wet's office was on the second floor of the administration building. There was a view of the passenger terminal buildings with the uniformed figures on top, a chain of soldiers before the parking apron, a guard of honour already assembled, a flag-decked reviewing stand. Vision faded up on the TV monitors, three pictures showing different aspects of the same story: uniforms everywhere. Men in plain clothes too. You could tell who belonged to the Executive Protection Service: it didn't matter which way their bodies pointed, their eyes were always some-where else.

"My guess is the helicopter is not going to be used for an attack."

"Guesses…" The breath sighed out of him.

"It's for the get-away."

"Then it will be shot down." De Wet was solid with com-placency. "The air force has been trained for just such an eventuality."

"They've thought of that. They've taken a young girl hostage. She'll be on board."

"*God verdomme.*"

The huge domed forehead creased in frowns. The existence of a hostage had introduced a discordant moral element.

I said: "You're beginning to believe me. You no longer dis-count everything I say."

He thought about that and took refuge in self-satisfaction.

"It is my job to evaluate information. How do you know about the girl hostage?"

"She is the daughter of the diamond broker Poelsma."

"I know the name. Your story is unlikely: there has been no alert for a kidnapping."

"Poelsma is a sympathizer…"

"Now you are being ridiculous." He smoothed a hand across the dome where only a short time ago there had been hair. Maybe he was forty, a podgy captain at forty, at the limit of his promo-tion because he was good at organizing guards of honour and searching baggage.

"He is a sympathizer of Blood Group O, who have him turned into an activist by kidnapping his daughter. It is my belief he is being forced to mount the assassination, to show he is more than a weak bourgeois radical."

"How does he propose to go about it?"

"I don't know how."

He made a little noise, dropping his pipe on the desk. I'd lost him again. He kept half-believing, then finding me ridiculous. "He's just flown in from Tel Aviv. Ring El Al. Check the passenger list."

Instead de Wet stood by the window. The angle of the building gave us a partial view of the huge parking apron with its clutter of commercial jets, fuel tankers, catering vans. The El Al Boeing 707 had been guided into a vacant berth and passengers were coming through the forward exit. It was far too distant to recognize faces. The first man down stood at the bottom of the steps checking the baggage-handlers who were opening the underbelly. No airline operates stricter security than El Al.

It nagged me. If no airline operated stricter security than El Al, why had Poelsma flown to Israel; why choose El Al to return on? There'd be a reason. Possibility: the airline knew he was a courier for French Security and granted him special facilities. Likelihood: zero. An airline knows nothing: only individuals can have knowledge and once the knowledge you are a courier begins to spread, your usefulness is at an end.

De Wet shook his head. "No, Miss Cody. Let us assume Poelsma flew in from Tel Aviv on that plane. What do you imagine he could do? He couldn't carry any weapon. Have you any idea of the security arrangements at Ben Gurion airport? They'd confiscate my pipe cleaners. This story is part of your imagination. This young Dutchman with the motorbike—he is someone who picked you up? A new boy friend? You thought this would add a touch of excitement to your romance?"

"For Christ's sake." I stopped. I caught the rising inflection in my voice and it was no good his dismissing me as a hysterical female. "You know Blood Group O sympathizers are planning a rally. I bet they're coming in busloads from Germany in support. Suppose, just for a moment, no terrorism is planned here. Suppose Poelsma simply has a briefcase of propaganda leaflets to hurl in the air. Suppose one of your men is trigger-happy and mistakes Poelsma's gestures and guns him down. If even a trivial incident occurs and I gave you warning about it, will Comissaris Bosch be pleased?"

He swung round abruptly to look at me. Bosch was the name at the head of the distribution list on the file. His gaze flickered away to the young officer who stood back in the room and then to me. "How do you know Commissaris Bosch?"

"It doesn't matter. What matters is this: it could be a demonstration, a messy suicide mission, a full-blooded terrorist attack from the air, and I have given you advance warning. Are you going to tell Bosch you ignored it?" There would be something inside that domed forehead. He had to operate on some principle, even if it were only bending the knee before his superior. "When is the plane due in now?"

He kept his eyes locked on me, moved very stiffly to the squawkbox and depressed the switch.

"Give me Voice." He breathed heavily as he waited. "Blue Cat, do you read? Captain de Wet OOH/5. When is Air Force One due in?"

"Checked past Haarlem on final approach. Touchdown in two hundred ten seconds."

"Roger copy, Blue Cat." De Wet had been playing with the boys long enough to learn the language.

The dimensions of the problem were now precisely defined. Physically: here in this office with a Security Captain who was sceptical; and outside where an assassin had flown in from Israel and the American President's aircraft was in its final approach. Defined also in time: three and a half minutes.

Still de Wet wouldn't credit me with bringing him an accurate warning. He was just taking out insurance, in case of the unexpected.

It was no use trying to convince de Wet on anything except purely practical grounds: that despite massive security an assassination operation was at that moment being mounted against the President of the United States. A man with more imagination, a man like Crevecoeur, would take precautions simply because of possible wider implications.

Total peace might not be an attainable goal because there were too many who would not accept it. A generation had been raised in distrust and deprivation and hatred. But there was a chance the next generation would grow up in more hope and Crevecoeur would see that. If a form of co-existence were achieved in the Middle East then it was possible money would no longer be swallowed by the eaters of steel. Instead of machines of war, there would be tractors and houses and schools.

A dream, but better than a nightmare.

De Wet was never a man who would dream.

I looked out of the window again. They were unrolling the red carpet: they had kept it under cover in case of further rain squalls. I looked west, towards the North Sea and America, but nothing showed, just grey cumulus scudding across the blue. A service road ran directly behind the reviewing stand with its Stars and Stripes and the orange, white and blue of the Dutch flag. A squat green pick-up truck with no windows in its body drove down the road. Nobody paid it any attention: it had already passed through the security checkpoint.

I watched the green truck and it curved past a British Airways Trident and braked by the El Al Boeing. Two men in helmets got out.

"What is that truck, the green one?"

De Wet glanced down. "Security transport. Obligatory when anything valuable is being moved."

"Like diamonds?"

"Yes."

I was no longer looking out of the window. The scene was showing on a TV monitor as one of the cameras scanned the parking apron. Two men stood under the belly of the El Al jet supervising the unloading of a heavy metal box. The one who wasn't the El Al security guard was Poelsma. The screen showed only a monochrome picture but the features and the curls were unmistakable.

Then I knew it, what Blood Group O planned, its precision and ingenuity, why they had brought pressure to bear on Poelsma, the reason for the El Al flight, the part of the helicopter. I knew the how.

There were two minutes left.

"De Wet, you said you knew the security procedures at Tel Aviv: do they search baggage?"

"Of course. Baggage and body checks. Metal detectors, X-ray, visual and hand searches. Most thorough."

"De Wet, listen very closely because the seconds are ticking away."

He turned to me, the light glistening on his domed forehead.

"Poelsma is a man they know well, respected, a frequent traveller, always maintaining the tightest security when he escorts his highly valuable shipment of diamonds. Possibly he even arrives at Tel Aviv airport in an armoured vehicle with guards, loading *directly* into the security hold of the aircraft … "

I saw something crumple inside him: it was the belief in himself. One moment his self-regard had been impregnable, and of a sudden it came crashing down in ruins. It showed in his eyes and the jigging of his Adam's apple.

I went on: "The box is too valuable to be checked out on the airport apron at Tel Aviv. Anyway, what need is there? Poelsma is there, accompanying the consignment. Poelsma signs papers, like he's done a couple of dozen times before, fills in export declaration forms for the customs, cracks a joke, asks the pilot to drop him off at the Sixteenth arrondissement as they fly over Paris. If there is sweat on his forehead, that is because the sun is hot. No more. Poelsma climbs on board. Nobody has checked what is inside the box. And that is why Blood Group O needed Poelsma."

De Wet brooded at the monitor and I turned my back on him so that the agony of his reappraisal would be unregarded. I looked out of the window. The box stood on the concrete by the back of the truck. I looked away to the west: the service road the armoured pick-up took passed directly behind the podium where the President would stand. The explosive charge in the box would be radio-activated, controlled by Poelsma: he gripped a black attaché case.

There were a lot of variable factors: type of explosive, quantity, construction of the metal container, position within the armoured truck, thickness of the armour plating, strength of the lock and hinges. At a rough estimate it would annihilate the American President, the Dutch Premier, the American ambassador, all officials on the reviewing stand, with the blast damage spreading out through the ranks of the military band and the guard of honour.

In the confusion the helicopter would sweep in and pluck Poelsma to safety. Nobody at that juncture would suspect him.

Beyond the airport I could see the glint of sun on an aircraft, very low, undercarriage down, on the final approach path. Above it was an escort of three Starfighters.

I looked back at the monitor. Poelsma seemed to be arguing with somebody and then he turned back to the aircraft steps.

De Wet faced the monitor, his eyes glazed. He couldn't bring himself to acknowledge that I was right and that the whole caravanserai of Security was hopelessly inadequate. The enormity of the step he was being asked to take was too great.

"Poelsma is too early, de Wet. Air Force One hasn't touched down yet. He's gone back on board for his hat or a book or something. No, he'll have said he's mislaid the customs manifest and when he judges the time right he'll wave the truck on. Look where it's going to drive."

De Wet jerked his head to the west, the road past the reviewing stand. Beyond it, much larger now, was the President's plane, sinking towards the end of the runway. De Wet was sweating profusely as his brain strained to absorb the flood of information, to make sense out of a world suddenly gone mad. He checked back at the apron: there was no sign of Poelsma but the box was being slid into the back of the truck.

"De Wet, he's coming from Tel Aviv. Have you considered he might have chosen there because the Israelis have developed nuclear weapons?"

A tremor began in one of his hands.

"How do you know?"

"Why else would the Egyptians be back looking for peace?"

He had gone very white.

It was no good because I was running out of time. De Wet lacked the imagination and it was as simple as that. He could not accept that I was right and he wrong. So I put it to him in the only terms that had a chance of success now: because preservation of self is the most basic human drive.

I said: "If that's a nuclear device, don't stand by the window. You'll be in line for a high radiation dose."

When he moved, he was quick.

"Give me Voice. De Wet OOH/5. This is a red alert, repeat red alert. First priority, most immediate, Air Force One to overfly, repeat, Air Force One to overfly. Second priority, suspected explosive device off-loaded from El Al plane on to green security pick-up. Isolate the truck and detain passenger by name Poelsma, incoming Tel Aviv. Third priority, flash all posts to monitor possible adverse helicopter. Confirm, Blue Cat."

The deep mid-West voice was unflustered. "Captain de Wet, you do not have the seniority to authorize an overflight. You must obtain the agreement of your Commissaris Bosch."

"Blue Cat, you must understand this is a full alert condition. I have received evidence of terrorist activity here in the red carpet area."

There was the look of a caged animal on de Wet's face. Panic for his own safety had driven him to believe. He wanted to break loose, run out to the apron and hurl the metal box far away.

"Captain de Wet, the Joint Control Agreement…"

"There is no time for all this bloody protocol."

The Presidential jet's wheels touched the runway at 3.14. It showed on the second TV monitor and a voice said: "Affirmative touchdown."

Sweat filmed de Wet's forehead, a pulse throbbed in his throat.

"Captain de Wet, security control of the red carpet area is the joint responsibility of the Dutch Royal Militia and our Executive Protection Service. Unless you have…"

"And where was your damn Executive Protection Service in Dallas in November 1963?"

"Hold one moment, Captain de Wet."

There was a blur of other voices from the sqawkbox and someone was shrilling, "Abort, I don't give a hard shit, get him the hell out." And then the unflustered mid-Westerner said: "We have a problem, Captain de Wet, an intruder over the wire at Orange Sector Three. Reported Alouette helicopter."

"Blue Cat, that is definitely a hostile intruder but there is a hostage being held on board."

"Read you, Captain."

De Wet wiped the palms of both hands on a handkerchief and dabbed at the high dome. The shine of sweat returned almost at once.

He said: "How stable are these people? I mean, will they take vengeance if they are thwarted?"

I said: "They are not open to rational argument. They have closed minds. And there's no time to call in the psychiatrists."

"What will they do to their hostage on the helicopter when their operation is blocked?"

We stared at the row of TV monitors. One showed a Lincoln Continental gliding up to the reviewing stand. Plain clothes men jogged beside it. On the second the camera panned as the Boeing 707 with Air Force One on its side hurtled down the runway and I suddenly grasped that the plane wasn't going to stop; the runway had some four kilometres of usable length and about two-thirds of the way along the wheels unstuck and the plane was airborne again.

"What'll they do?" he repeated.

"I wish I could tell you." It frightened me and not just for young Simone's safety. The pressure was immense on one man, and with his daughter threatened by wholly unexpected developments I feared he would fall over the edge.

The third monitor was on the parking apron and the camera did an abrupt zoom on the El Al jet. A face showed at one of the portholes, grey, expressionless, anonymous. The face turned and we saw what had caught his attention.

"Marines," de Wet said. "They've had experience in this sort of situation. The Hague, Assen."

De Wet was wrong. The Marines had no experience of a situation like this. Twice they'd been sent in at Assen to rescue hostages from Moluccan terrorists but only after protracted negotiations had weakened the terrorists' resolve and after meticulous planning and at times of their own choosing and against reluctant martyrs. Here they were acting against a man of doubtful stability, whose mind was teetering between self-preservation and the saving of his daughter's life.

Faced with a choice like that, a crescendo of doubts and fears and conflicting demands, a mind does the only thing it can: it takes refuge in insanity. And Marines cannot get inside an insane mind.

They came in four jeeps, screaming across the apron, and the first of them were running up the steps to the forward cabin of the El Al jet when the scene went berserk.

Television accustoms us to images of violence and it could have been another late night movie except that the flash on the screen was matched by the flicker of orange reflected on the ceiling of our office. We felt the blast. Then the music of war boomed across the concrete apron.

On the screen was a billowing cloud of dust and thick smoke and through it I could make out the payload portion of the armoured security truck still intact but the doors were blown off. The armoured walls had vented the blast back at the aircraft and there were holes ripped in its underbelly and nearside wing. The cowling had been torn clean off the nearest engine pod. The portable steps were swept away. Marines lay twisted on the concrete, and then came the fireball as the aviation kerosene took flame.

It went up with a thump, overwhelming, drowning the cries of the men on the ground.

I walked to the window, a helpless spectator, the bloody mess mocking the efforts I'd made to stop it.

A couple of figures dropped from the gaping airliner door and scrambled up and ran, trailing flames from their clothes. Marines were dragging wounded comrades clear. Men and vehicles made an aimless pattern, racing to and away from the blazing plane. The military band by the reviewing stand was marching away in good order; nobody was interested in national anthems now.

There was a clamour from ambulances and fire tenders. Somewhere an alarm siren wailed for the dead.

The Presidential jet banked away, leaving a dirty trail in the sky.

Shock takes people in strange ways. I thought Captain de Wet's shoulders were heaving with sobs until I heard the laughter.

CHAPTER TWENTY-FOUR

LOOSDRECHTSCHE PLASSEN
FRIDAY 23 MARCH
9.45 P.M.

He took the clothes off me slowly, his face intent, almost grave. He was clumsy with the zip on the slacks but the tremor was natural: the first time with someone there is a tingle that communicates itself to the fingers. We kissed. He'd had his mouth on mine when he'd taken me out of the lake during the day but this had a different significance. Our lips and tongues explored and I had my hands in his hair. And when I looked up in his eyes they were still serious. It haunted him.

I said: "It's because I was wearing her clothes, isn't it?"

We don't like the notion of someone else haunting a person's mind at an intimate moment. Joop's smile was small, lopsided.

He pulled me close to his chest and ran a hand down my back. His fingers were blunt and firm on my skin.

"You feel good," he said.

I wasn't happy with the idea of his making love to another woman through my body. He felt the tension.

"It's not what you think," he said. He held me by the shoulders so he could search my face. "My ship has been on the run to Japan and it's the first time I've been back to the cabin since she left. Maybe we never had a chance because I am sometimes away three or four months at a time. But that wasn't what she said."

I could have turned my face aside thougn his grip on my shoulders was tight. The bluntness of his fingers was matched by the bluntness of his approach. He was honest and direct where another man would have pulled the shutters over the past at a time like this.

"When she left it was for a painter in Amsterdam. Another woman. She told me it had been a revelation, the true nature of her sexuality. Maybe that was so. Maybe it was right for her. But Co, the thought remains, was I really so bad with her? To lose a woman to a man is painful, but let's say it is the luck of the dice. To lose a woman to another woman..."

He couldn't think of the words to finish.

And perhaps he'd had a run ashore at Yokohama or Macao or Singapore but that wouldn't reassure him: the words he'd hear would be insincere, the gestures mechanical. It was his confidence in his masculinity that was shaken.

And so I moved my hands over him and ran my fingers down his spine and curved over his hip and circled his navel and felt the tight curls and as we stood with our bodies clinging together I took my mouth off his and said: "I think you're somebody special."

He caught my hair in one hand and pulled my head back. He kissed my throat and breasts. He bit at the lobe of an ear. He ran his tongue over my lips and our mouths closed again. I could feel the urgency in him and I wanted him with the same intensity because it had been a day with hate and death and pain and suffering. I wanted to lose myself in one other human being and know there was pleasure we could give to one another and not violence.

He said: "And I think you're sexy. But I expect a lot of men tell you that."

I shivered.

"What is it?"

"I'm cold. Let's get into bed."

But it was a different sort of cold. The last person who'd told me I was sexy was Yussif. I had encouraged him. And then I had killed him. It wasn't a thought I could share.

CHAPTER TWENTY-FIVE

WITTEHUIS
SATURDAY 24 MARCH
00.20 A.M.

Joop had an arm across me and as I slipped from under it he stirred but didn't waken. I fingered a crack between the curtains and looked over the lake. Lights shone from the house on the island. The sound didn't repeat itself, the sound that had alerted me, distant, like someone cracking his knuckles far off.

I'd thought Wittehuis was deserted. Possibly the lights had been on all the time but my attention had been on Joop.

I dressed and went to Joop's boathouse. He'd said he had a *bijboot* and that turned out to be a dinghy with an Evinrude outboard motor. I used the oars because I didn't want to advertise my arrival. The breath clouded before me in the cold air. The moon was half full and it came from behind the clouds and spangled on the water. The light-track Wittehuis threw on the lake was like a cruise liner passing at sea.

I felt lost in the little dinghy, alone in the night.

I tied the boat up and nobody was waiting in the concrete pillbox or the shadows beside the path.

Light seeped out at the bottom of the heavy curtains drawn in the living room but I could see clearly into the other rooms: dining room, a booklined study, a utility room, the kitchen. One of the kitchen windows was unlatched: its hinge needed oil.

A house absorbs the character of the people who live there. The atmosphere can be overpowering: of happiness or loneliness or tension, of a family that has grown and left and the house no longer has a function. Wittehuis was dead.

Kitchen, utility room, dining room, hall. Nothing.

I opened the door to the living room and the smell was a shock. I caught the aroma of *tabac noir* before I saw him. He was slumped in a chair, morose, tight-faced, looking as drained as I felt.

"So." Crevecoeur sighed.

The television set was on, a ghost screen shining grey and empty, and I went and switched it off. He'd made me do it again, perform some petty domestic act for him. I felt a spurt of resentment and I nourished it because anger brings alertness.

"No, don't do that," Crevecoeur said. "Turn it on again. There's something you might like to see."

"There are no programmes. It's too late."

"We have the late show." His lips stretched across his teeth in a thin smile as he got to his feet. "He was a rich man, van Berkel. A rich and successful lawyer. He had a rich man's toys."

There was a Philips video cassette recorder on the shelf behind the TV set. Crevecoeur rewound the tape and switched on the set.

"I was looking at this before you came. Van Berkel had made a video recording of the news."

The news broadcast on TV-1 had been extended to cover the afternoon's events at Amsterdam airport, the delayed arrival of the political leaders, and the final act with the helicopter.

At 7.45 the helicopter had spiralled in to land at Copenhagen airport. On board were Mogens, Cathy, Vratko and the hostage, young Simone Poelsma. I couldn't follow the newscaster's Dutch but some of the negotiations were included and they were in English. Mogens was adamant about a DC8, fuelled up, engines running.

"No crew." His voice came thin on the helicopter's radio. "No crew, d'you hear?"

"How will you fly her?"

"I have training with the DC8."

"You cannot fly her solo."

"Nobody else. Don't you understand? Nobody else. We don't trust anybody. No tricks, no cops in SAS uniforms. You hear me, do you…"

"Okay, okay."

I glanced at Crevecoeur and he was watching intently, though he'd seen it before. Perhaps there was satisfaction on his face.

It was Vratko who held a Walther sub-machine gun to Simone's head as they walked to the aircraft. It was parked in isolation, in an area of nothing, and the shadows of the four moving figures loomed large in front. There were jeeps and armed soldiers at the extremities of the floodlit apron. Nobody moved to stop them. They started to climb the movable steps to the DC8. The little girl clung to Cathy's hand as they mounted and Cathy bent down to speak to her.

Mogens went in first and passed through to the flight deck. Vratko was swinging the door into place and at the last moment Cathy pushed the nine-year-old girl out through the gap. Simone tumbled to the concrete and lay there crying, her little white face wrapped around the sobs.

Vratko succeeded in shutting the door. Mogens started taxiing the aircraft. It must have taken fully fifteen or twenty seconds for the army to realize they were no longer constrained by a hostage and then the tyres were shot out. The plane slewed to a halt. The news broadcast showed images of soldiers running, an armoured car advancing, of a man firing from the aircraft door before toppling to the ground. A grenade exploded though it was unclear whether it had been hurled from inside or outside the plane. Finally there was a crowd of uniformed figures surrounding the aircraft while stretchers were rolled into the back of an ambulance.

"They died," Crevecoeur said simply. "If that doll-faced young woman hadn't pushed their hostage out, they'd have got away. In effect she killed them."

There was a final picture of Simone with shorn hair and pinched cheeks. She looked as if she had never in her life chased through fields and laughed at the sun.

Crevecoeur got up to switch off the VCR. He peered for a moment at the eerie nothing of the TV screen and switched that off too.

"I should thank you," he said, formally, not turning round.

"I don't want thanks."

"Not my thanks. I should thank you on behalf of my department, my government. If Blood Group O had succeeded in assassinating any one of those political leaders, there would have been more bloodshed than that, more repression, more violence, more martyrs."

"Crevecoeur, look at me."

He turned.

"How did you know to come here?" I asked.

"The security people."

I shook my head. The chaos at Amsterdam airport had been total. Joop and I had left without telling anyone about Wittehuis.

"Not the circus they had at the airport," he said. "You forget I do a lot of liaison with West German Security. Do you know they have a computer at Wiesbaden with a program on international terrorism: imprisoned terrorists, associates, suspects still at large, descriptions, sympathizers, foreign connections, houses, bank accounts, printing presses, lawyers, working methods, weapons used, disguises, so forth. You know, I like computers." He spoke with a certain shyness, a man confessing an intimate secret. If he liked computers it was because he foresaw some more perfect method of control in the future. "The computer gave out thirty-four names of potential activist members of Blood Group O. We asked a number of questions about safe houses and curiously this one wasn't in the store-core. We got no further with arms suppliers either. But with legal advisers the name van Berkel appeared, and he'd also done some work for the Poelsma diamond firm, so we had a connection. At van Berkel's office his secretary said he'd taken a week's vacation and come here. So ... " He shrugged.

He'd talked too much. When he stopped he lit another Gitane, frowning, realizing he was using too many words, trying to obscure something.

"When did you find out about Blood Group O?"

He studied me through the smoke. "Behind that question, Cody, is the suggestion that I could have issued you some warning, or got here sooner than I did."

Yes. It had entered my mind that he intended I would be killed, even from the start that had been his hope, because I knew one little fact about him: on one occasion at least in the past he had co-operated with the East Germans. Such a tiny thing. There is liaison in surprising matters between East and West, but they hate it to be known.

I said: "Why aren't there any other personnel from the Sûreté here? Or Dutch Security? Why do you always work alone?"

He stared at me with his unnaturally pale eyes.

"Cody, what do you mean?"

I think I meant: Why do you never have witnesses to your actions? Why isn't there a crowd of cops trampling the tulip beds? Why is there nobody who can report your words? Are you just another of the *copains et coquins* adjusting the world to your liking? My unease was too vague to be put into precise words.

"Cody, you've been through a lot, you're overtired. I would never risk Blood Group O assassinating the American President. Admit that."

He was right: I was too tired to think clearly. Maybe he'd been running ragged trying to track down the terrorists. Maybe he'd kept away from the airport for a different reason. I'd worry about it when I'd slept.

"And Ulrike?" I asked. "She wasn't on the helicopter."

"You're as full of questions as a cop." He tried his smile and suddenly I was sick of him. I started to walk away. There were still some hours of the night left and I had a friend to return to. I could still feel the imprint of his lips.

Crevecoeur's words stopped me half way to the door. "All of them are finished. The whole group. Ulrike and van Berkel are in a bedroom upstairs. They used pistols, a suicide pact."

I swung round to face him. "That's very…" My tired brain fought for a word. "Neat? Convenient?"

Crevecoeur frowned. "I cannot help that. You're not suggesting I had a hand in it?"

We looked at each other in silence. There was the feeling, almost tangible, of the whole house holding its breath. Indeed for all I knew the kitchen might be stuffed with French *paras* who'd stormed their way in.

"Why did Ulrike stay behind?" I asked. Van Berkel I could understand—he was only a rich bourgeois sympathizer. But Ulrike was the strong one—she should have been in the heat of the action.

Crevecoeur slumped lower in the chair and I thought for a time he wasn't going to answer. It's hard to share secrets in their shadow world. "You understand," he said, "that the assassination was intended as a *coup de propagande* against the imperialists. That's us." The thin smile again, fleetingly. "For Ulrike, the only German left among them, it would be doubly powerful: redeeming the Stammheim pledge."

I shook my head. He had lost me.

"Eighteen months ago three German terrorists killed themselves in Stammheim prison. They left a suicide note which grew into something of a legend. It even boasted a legendary sort of name: *das Blut-Brief.* The Blood Letter was never published, of course, but whispers got out. It had prophesied revenge and the assassination at Amsterdam airport was to be the bloody fulfilment of that. Ulrike, the only German-speaker, had a role no one else would play. There was a sheet of paper, a statement in German, by her body, and among the revolutionary cries there was talk of *Blut-Brief* and Stammheim and *Kamaraden.* Also she had a list of telephone numbers, newspapers in Bonn, Cologne, Stuttgart, so on. Let us assume she intended to utter her revolutionary manifesto to the German press at the height of Blood Group O's triumph when it would have maximum impact. Instead they failed. She even watched the failure on television." He made a meaningless little gesture. "And she killed herself."

"Where is the statement?"

He pointed at the pile of grey ash in the ashtray. "We don't want to create any more mythology."

"You can't choke a myth so easily," I said. Legends prosper in the shadows, surely he understood that. "There'll be a rumour that the security police killed Ulrike and her lover."

"You mean me?" He shrugged. "But I've never been here."

He went to the desk and opened the second drawer down. He knew just where the envelopes were kept. He tipped the ash into one, went on to the ashtray he'd been using for his Gitanes and emptied the butts. He tucked the envelope into an inside pocket.

"Every active member of Blood Group O has now died," he said.

"Poelsma?"

"Poelsma. It is sad about Poelsma. I was so sure of him. Shall I tell you why? His father was shot by the SS in Holland in 1943 for hiding Jews and British pilots. Poelsma's father was one of the minor heroes of the Resistance; they even named a street after him in Amsterdam. It is odd how viewpoints change with the generations. The father sheltered Jews but the son associated with people who wanted to murder Jews: they separated the Jews out at Entebbe and Mogadishu. The father fought against dictatorship but the son tried to assassinate a leader who is freely elected. Don't you find that an irony?"

He stopped. He spoke with the precision of a teacher in a lycée and I thought he'd finished. It was quiet in the room. I went to the door, had my fingers on the knob.

"You saw that picture of little Simone Poelsma on television," Crevecoeur said. He was reluctant to let me go. "She looked like someone who'd been rescued from Belsen. She'd taken part in events that will scar her for life: the kidnapping, being held at gunpoint with the searchlights on her, her father burned to death. Nine years old."

A floorboard creaked outside and I opened the door. There was nothing, nobody. It was just the dead house.

"How will she react when she grows up?" Crevecoeur asked. "I wonder what Blood Group she belongs to?"

On the path down to the boat a rat scuttled away into the dark.